THE

POWER
Is it
a gift—
or a
curse?

The Fear Experiment

by Jesse Harris

Borzoi Sprinters · Alfred A. Knopf · New York

A BORZOI SPRINTER PUBLISHED BY ALFRED A. KNOPF, INC.
Copyright © 1992 by Parachute Press, Inc.
Cover photograph © 1992 by Andrew Moore

Library of Congress Cataloging-in-Publication Data
Harris, Jesse.
The fear experiment / by Jesse Harris.
p.   cm.—(The Power ; bk. #3)
"Borzoi sprinters."
Summary: Handsome Dr. Chaney, a visiting teacher, endangers the
lives of high school students, including that of psychic McKenzie
Gold, when he carries his hypnosis experiments a step too far.
ISBN 0-679-82266-6 (pbk.) — ISBN 0-679-92266-0 (lib. bdg.)
[1. Hypnotism—Fiction.   2. Extrasensory perception—Fiction.
3. Teachers—Fiction.   4. High schools—Fiction.   5. Schools—
Fiction.] I. Title. II. Series: Harris, Jesse. Power ; bk. #3.
PZ7.H2419Fe   1992   [Fic]—dc20   91-20788

RL: 5.7
First Borzoi Sprinter edition: May 1992

Manufactured in the United States of America
10 9 8 7 6 5 4 3 2 1

chapter 1

The rope. The moment McKenzie walked into the gym, she saw it. The rope was thick and bristly, with a large knot tied at the bottom. It ran all the way up to the highest point in the ceiling—above the basketball scoreboard.

"No way," McKenzie told Lilicat. "They can't make *me* climb that thing."

Her best friend was busy doing warmup stretches; Lilicat's shoulder-length dark hair hung straight down toward the floor as she bent over to touch her toes. "Relax, wouldja?" she said, still upside down. "We're supposed to play volleyball today, remember?"

Volleyball? McKenzie peered around the room. Girls in white T-shirts and blue shorts were still straggling in. "The net's not even up," she moaned. "They're going to make us climb it. I know it. What am I going to do?"

"Climb it. It's not that bad."

Not for Lilicat. But all her life, McKenzie had had a terrible fear of heights. She couldn't even watch someone on TV walk out on a ledge or dangle from a cliff. She squinted up at the top of the rope, then looked away quickly.

Brrrrreeep! A shrill whistle blast made her jump. "Okay, everybody!" yelled their gym teacher, Ms. Lyons. "Line up!"

"Maybe I could say I have the flu," McKenzie whispered.

Lilicat smiled at her kindly. "Don't worry. We're going to play volleyball. I promise you."

"Instead of volleyball, today we're going to take a fitness exam," barked Ms. Lyons. McKenzie gave her friend a dirty look.

"What do you want?" Lilicat said under her breath. "*I'm* not the one with ESP."

"We start with chin-ups," Ms. Lyons told them. "Then push-ups, sit-ups, then vaulting, and a fifty-yard dash. Last but not least, we come over here and"—Ms. Lyons pointed toward the scoreboard—"we climb the rope."

McKenzie felt her stomach turn over. My face is probably green, she thought. Ms. Lyons picked five team captains and told them to choose up sides. One of the captains was Lilicat.

Not too surprising. Lilicat was on the cheerleading team. Her flips and splits were famous, and she was pretty good at all sports. Unlike McKenzie. Right now the only event McKenzie wanted to enter was sprinting—straight home!

For her first pick, Lilicat chose McKenzie. "Big mistake," McKenzie told her, trotting over to stand next to her friend. "There's no way I'm going to make it up that rope."

"You'll be fine, Mack. Trust me. Have I ever led you astray?"

"Are we playing volleyball?"

Their team won the push-up competition, beating out Jane Ewing's team by three. Not bad, considering that Jane was a great athlete and the school's diving champion. McKenzie felt a little better. She had forced herself past her usual limit of ten push-ups all the way to fifteen. Those extra ones had made a big difference.

As the test continued, she couldn't help sneaking glances at the rope. It looked like an instrument of torture. Maybe she could explain to Ms. Lyons about her fear of heights.

But Ms. Lyons kept blowing her whistle, marking her clipboard, checking her stopwatch, and yelling instructions. Then Martina Braswell, who was about twenty pounds overweight, asked her if she could be excused from climbing the rope. Ms. Lyons ordered her to go back to her team. So much for talking to Ms. Lyons.

After four events, the score was still close. McKenzie had started to sweat, and not from the exercise. Maybe, she thought, I should just fall over during the fifty-yard dash. That way the score won't be close and I won't have to climb the rope.

But she ran fast. They raced five at a time, and McKenzie came in second in her group.

"See," Lilicat told her, "I *was* smart to pick you for my team." McKenzie gasped for breath.

Ms. Lyons blew her whistle. "At the end of five events," she announced, "we have a two-way tie for first between Lilith's team and Jane's. The rest of you aren't far behind." As she read off the scores, she reached for the stopwatch that hung around her neck. "It all comes down to how fast you can get up and down this rope."

"You okay?" Lilicat asked McKenzie. McKenzie smiled and nodded. But her legs were rubbery. She was beginning to feel nauseated. The fear she had felt so far was nothing compared with what she was experiencing now. It was coming in waves. Let our team go last, she prayed. And let the bell ring in time. Please.

"We'll start with Lilith's team. McKenzie Gold? It's your turn to go first."

Her team let out a cheer. Taking a deep breath, she walked over to the rope. The rope's heavy knotted bottom lay in a coil on a pile of thick red mats. She stepped up onto the mats, then reached out and grabbed the thick rope with both hands. Her palms were sweating terribly.

"You can do it, Mack!" yelled Lilicat.

"On your mark!" cried Ms. Lyons, studying her stopwatch. "Get set . . . *go!*"

McKenzie jumped up and grabbed the rope, reaching with one arm after another, shinnying upward as fast as she could. Don't look down, she ordered herself. Don't look down!

"Thatta baby!" someone screamed from down below. She was going higher. Everyone was shouting.

And then she made a fatal mistake. She glanced down to see how far she had come.

The answer was, she had come far enough to make the drop to the floor below look terrifying. The upturned faces of her classmates had gotten noticeably smaller.

Don't look! she screamed at herself, but now she couldn't tear her gaze away. The room began to spin below her. She felt dizzy, sick to her stomach. She looked away, but it was too late. She was frozen.

Fear gripped her body. The screaming from below was growing louder. She shut her eyes. The clock was running. But it was no use—she couldn't move at all, up or down. Her arms were getting so incredibly tired. She couldn't hold on much longer. Move! she commanded herself.

She did move, but not up. Her sweaty hands slipped down several inches, the bristly rope burning her palms. Then one hand lost its grip altogether, and she swung away from the rope.

A loud gasp rose to greet her from down below. She tried to regain control, clutching for the rope with her free hand. But the force of gravity was pulling her down, down, prying her fingers off the rope. She felt her hand let go.

She was falling. Red mats zoomed toward her, kids' faces suddenly grew huge. And then . . . everything faded to black.

chapter 2

Still wearing her gym uniform, McKenzie sat in the waiting room of the school nurse's office, gingerly massaging her bruised elbow. Lucky for her, the thick mats had cushioned her fall.

Lilicat stuck her head in the door and asked, "How's the patient?" Along with Ms. Lyons, she had convinced McKenzie to go see the nurse; in fact, she had insisted on escorting her there herself. She had left only when it was time for French.

"Fine, except I'm still embarrassed."

When she fell, McKenzie had blacked out—very briefly—but she had blacked out nonetheless. Nurse Dockett wasn't taking any chances.

She had made her stick around for an hour now, keeping her "under supervision."

"Our mini starts in about fifteen minutes," Lilicat reminded her. "I hope you're feeling up to it. Jane Ewing ran into the teacher in the principal's office at lunch. She says he's *hot*."

McKenzie smiled. "I feel better already."

Lakeville Senior High had started special three-week courses for juniors and seniors known as minis. Juniors this year, McKenzie and Lilicat now qualified; they had both signed up for a double mini in psychology.

Lilicat had signed up so that they'd have at least one class together. McKenzie had signed up because she wanted to learn everything she could about how the mind worked. Especially *her* mind.

Lilicat was one of the only people in the world who was aware of it, but McKenzie had psychic abilities. Her sleep was sometimes troubled by strange visions. And when she woke up in the morning, she occasionally found that these visions—whether scary or beautiful—had actually happened.

Her parents first noticed her unusual abilities when she was a child. She began having nightmares and waking dreams, so they took her to a psychologist for testing. But the psychologist couldn't find the cause of the trouble, and after a while the nightmares passed. McKenzie's family simply got used to thinking of her as a little different.

But for McKenzie, the visions continued. From time to time unexpected images would overpower her—images of events happening right then but far away, images from the past or the future. She would lose sight of the world around her as her mind took her on a sudden journey. She had learned to pay close attention to these visions, to note every detail. What she saw always had some kind of meaning—even if the meaning wasn't clear to her at once.

Nurse Dockett emerged from her inner office. "Still feeling okay?" she asked.

McKenzie nodded.

"Good." She glanced at her watch. "There's not much time left in the day. I think we should send you home early."

"Home? I can't. I've got psychology! Please . . . I've been waiting for this for weeks."

Nurse Dockett frowned. "All right," she said finally, "but take it easy."

McKenzie hurried to the gym, showered, and changed back into her purple blouse and black jeans. She checked to make sure that her necklace—a crystal hanging from a gold chain—was still in place. It was a gift from her grandmother, and she never took it off. After she finished dressing, she headed for room 311.

The classroom usually belonged to Mr. Rodman, the geometry teacher. Multicolored geometric shapes hung from the ceiling, and there were still several theorems chalked up on the blackboard.

"Isn't it nice to be in here and not have to listen to a lecture about obtuse angles?" asked McKenzie, sitting down next to Lilicat.

English was McKenzie's favorite subject. Math was a bore.

The minute hand on the large, round wall clock ticked one notch: 2:00. The bell rang. The psychology teacher was late.

"No applause, please! Thank you! Thank you!"

McKenzie swiveled in her seat to watch senior Robb Sterfeld make his usual big entrance. He waved, acknowledged imaginary applause, and high-fived the outstretched hands of several of his swim team pals. His girlfriend, Jane Ewing, had walked in with him, but he was ignoring her. She sat down by herself.

Great, thought McKenzie. Just my luck that Robb Sterfeld has to be interested in psychology.

Now Robb walked up behind Paul Kelley's

desk. Paul, the class brain, was busy writing in his notebook and didn't see him. Robb grabbed Paul in a headlock and rubbed his knuckles on his head. "Just wanted to say hi to the brain," Robb said, letting go. His friends all laughed.

"Why don't you gr-gr-gr-gr-gr-grow up?" Paul stammered.

"Why don't you learn to ta-ta-ta-ta-talk?"

Just then, the door opened again. Everyone, including Robb, quickly took a seat. The room was quiet. Standing in the open doorway, finishing a conversation with Mr. Rodman, was a tall, handsome man with thick, wavy black hair. A dark, closely trimmed black beard showed off his powerful jaw line. Under his blue sports jacket and khakis his body appeared trim and muscular. He looked to be in his early thirties.

Lilicat and McKenzie exchanged glances. McKenzie's mouth dropped open. Jane hadn't been kidding around—the man *was* hot!

Whatever the new teacher was saying, it must have been funny. Mr. Rodman was guffawing. Then the new teacher laughed too. He even had a sexy laugh!

He closed the door, walked to the front of the room, put his leather attaché case on the desk, and snapped it open. "Hi. My name is

Dr. John Chaney," he said, flashing a dazzling smile.

McKenzie blinked—no, she wasn't dreaming.

"They tell me I'm supposed to teach you something about psychology. That's kind of a big subject to cover in six weeks. You see, psychology is known as the science of the mind. But it covers many different fields: everything from studying how rats find their way around mazes to understanding what makes humans fall in love."

I could answer that one, McKenzie thought. Thank goodness her boyfriend, Aidan, had calculus this period. He wouldn't appreciate watching her swoon.

"For instance, psychologists have found that the feeling of attraction may be triggered by smell." The class snickered.

"I know," he continued. "It's pretty shocking. You think you like some girl because she's nice or she's sexy and then the psychologists come along and tell you that you like her because of her B.O.!"

The class laughed; a few kids even clapped. Cool—he was the first teacher she remembered who had ever mentioned B.O.

Dr. Chaney's warm gaze settled on McKenzie. Their eyes locked.

"What did I tell you?" Lilicat whispered.

McKenzie shivered. She whispered back, "Wow!"

McKenzie's thoughts began to drift. "Hi, Mrs. Gold. I'm here to pick up McKenzie." Dr. Chaney was driving her to a fancy restaurant. They ate caviar and drank champagne at a candlelit table. They went for a moonlight stroll on the beach. . . .

The sound of John Chaney's deep voice brought her back to reality. "But I don't want to talk about any of that today. Today I want to start talking about the fun stuff: alternative mental states like sleepwalking, amnesia, and my personal fave—hypnosis."

McKenzie tried to let go of the picture of the beach and focus on what Dr. Chaney was saying. "You know," he went on, "hypnosis used to be dismissed by most of the scientific community as hocus-pocus. But today hypnosis has become a common and accepted practice. It's being used to cure everything from chronic back pain to warts."

Dr. Chaney found a piece of yellow chalk and wrote *hypnosis* on the board in big letters. Underneath he wrote *hypnos*.

"Hypnos was the Greek god of sleep. People used to think that hypnosis was like being asleep, because when you're in a trance, you look really out of it—glazed eyes, the whole bit. But scientists have measured the brain waves of people in trances and found they are hyper-alert."

Dr. Chaney moved away from the board and strolled in front of the class. "A lot of people are afraid of hypnosis because they think it's weird. But the fact is, you're all experiencing simple forms of trances every day. When you daydream in class, for instance—"

He moved in front of Bobby Beardsley's desk. Bobby was doodling in the margin of his notebook. Dr. Chaney slapped the notebook shut and Bobby jumped.

"That's a simple way to bring someone out of a trance," Dr. Chaney joked. He moved back to his desk. All eyes were on him now.

"The amazing thing, though—the fascinating and *bizarre* thing about trances is that when you're in one, you're very open to suggestion. That's why it's such a powerful—"

A hand shot up. McKenzie stared in amazement. It was Paul's. Usually Paul's goal in life was to avoid being noticed. "I thought it has been sh-sh-shown," he forced out, "that hyp-hyp-hypnosis doesn't really work."

"The only thing that doesn't really work,"

taunted Robb from the back of the room, "is your mou-mou-mou-mouth!"

Much to McKenzie's disgust, Robb's joke went over well with most of the class. But when they saw the look on Dr. Chaney's face, the students stopped laughing.

"Stand up," he told Robb calmly.

McKenzie swiveled in her seat to look at Robb. He stood, but defiantly.

"So what about you?" asked Dr. Chaney. "Do you believe in hypnosis?"

Robb shook his head. "It's a lot of baloney."

"I see. So it's nothing you'd ever be afraid of, right?"

Robb snorted. "Of course not."

"Great. Then you'd be willing to let someone try to hypnotize you?"

"Yeah." Robb raised an eyebrow to show that he was above it all, but he was starting to look a little uncomfortable.

Dr. Chaney clapped his hands. "Terrific. Thanks for volunteering. Come on up here."

McKenzie felt as if the room had suddenly taken on an electric charge. People were shifting in their seats as they looked back and forth at Robb and the teacher. She felt as if she were watching a tennis match.

"I said come up here. Now!" ordered Dr. Chaney. His manner didn't leave much room for argument. Robb swaggered to the front of the room. "Have a seat." The teacher pulled out a chair for him.

"Gosh," Robb said to his teammates, "isn't this exciting?" But he sat.

McKenzie glanced over at Paul. He was staring at Robb; his eyes had a dark glow.

Dr. Chaney towered above Robb. He rested his hand on Robb's shoulder. It looked as if he was holding him pretty firmly. But he spoke to Robb gently. He told Robb that he was right, there was nothing to be afraid of. He told him to close his eyes and relax.

"Let's start with your toes," Dr. Chaney said. "Focus on your toes and try to release any tension there."

With his eyes closed, Robb said, "You might as well know; I don't do anything on the first date!" Uproarious laughter erupted from the class.

But Dr. Chaney just said quietly, "Now your legs—let go of any tension. Feel them getting heavy. Think of warm Jell-O."

McKenzie leaned forward in her seat. She couldn't believe it. Was he actually going to *hypnotize* someone right now, right here, in front of everyone? She had always wanted to see this.

Robb was still making wisecracks, but he looked a lot more relaxed. His body was slumping forward slightly, and his head had begun to droop. Dr. Chaney sat down across from him. Soothingly, he told him that he was now going to put a finger on Robb's forehead. Robb was to focus on the pressure of his finger.

He pressed his index finger right in the middle of Robb's forehead. "Oh, Master," Robb intoned, "what is your command?"

Dr. Chaney smiled. "Just put all of your focus on my finger," he said, ignoring the joke. "Other thoughts will keep occurring to you, but whenever you notice that you're thinking of something else, put your focus back on my finger."

Dr. Chaney's soothing voice never stopped now as he continued to give Robb various instructions—to relax, to think of his body as heavier than lead, to think of all his worries floating away like a balloon. And all the time he kept his finger pressed on his forehead.

"Now I'm going to count down from ten. When I get to zero, you're going to be in a deep trance. And you'll remain in this deep trance until I snap my fingers. Understand?"

"Yeah."

"Now, when you're in this trance, you'll still be able to listen to me and answer my questions. You'll still be able to move around. But you'll know that everything I tell you is true. You won't have to question it. Understand?"

"Sure," Robb said, his eyes still closed.

Dr. Chaney began to count down. The class was very quiet. It seemed to McKenzie that Dr. Chaney was hypnotizing the whole room! ". . . Two . . . one . . . *zero*."

The teacher sat back, slowly taking his finger off the boy's forehead. Robb didn't move. Neither did anyone in the room.

"Okay, Robb," Dr. Chaney said, "you can open your eyes."

He opened them. But it didn't look like he was seeing anything; his eyes appeared glazed and unfocused.

"Robb?" Dr. Chaney asked.

"Yes?"

"What do you do after school?"

"After school? I have swim practice."

"Swim practice. I see. What time does that start?"

"Four thirty."

"Four thirty?" Dr. Chaney sounded surprised. "But it's four thirty now. You must be late."

"Uh-oh," Robb said. The class laughed again, but nervously. Robb was still goofing around, McKenzie thought. Or was he? His face looked like a mask. Robb now got to his feet.

"Where are you going?" Dr. Chaney asked.

"Swim practice. I'm late."

"Robb, you know better than that. You can't go into the pool like that. You've got to get into your swimsuit."

"Oh, you're right." Robb began to unbutton his shirt. There were shrieks from the class. Dr. Chaney signaled for quiet. Amazing, McKenzie thought. She never thought she'd see the day that Robb Sterfeld took orders from anyone.

Robb had now removed his red cotton shirt. Lucky for him, he had a T-shirt on underneath. But he reached down with both hands and pulled the T-shirt over his head. From the class came mock oohs and ahs.

At least Robb was in great shape. After hours of swimming, he had a bod worth showing off. But the class was laughing harder now. McKenzie couldn't believe her eyes. Robb reached down again—and began to unbuckle his pants!

chapter 3

Snap! Dr. Chaney snapped his fingers hard and loud and—

Immediately Robb stopped unbuckling his belt. Confused, he looked down at his naked torso and at his shirt and T-shirt lying on the floor. His mouth was slack. The laughter from the class came in a crash mixed with applause. Robb looked stunned. He knew they were not clapping for him.

"Wha—?"

"You can get dressed now," Dr. Chaney said, moving back behind the desk.

"I thought I was at swim practice," said Robb in a daze.

Paul was clapping louder than anyone else, laughing a high-pitched giggle and rocking back and forth in his seat with delight. "He got you, he got you! That's s-s-so cool!"

"You won't think it's so cool after I get *you*," Robb snarled, scooping up his clothes.

But no one was paying much attention to Robb anymore. All eyes were on Dr. Chaney.

"How did you do that?" Lumpy Johnson called out from the back.

"Is it hard to learn?"

"How does it work?" McKenzie found herself eagerly asking.

Dr. Chaney laughed and held up a hand. "One at a time." He explained that he'd been studying hypnosis on and off for years, with the help of research grants. Up until a few months ago he had been teaching at Marlboro University, just a few miles away, until his department had to make budget cutbacks.

"I'm sorry if I embarrassed you, Robb," he went on, "but I wanted to give you all a dramatic demonstration of the power of this tool. Think about it. Just by hypnotizing people and telling them not to focus on their physical pain, doctors can operate on people without using anesthesia! For people who are allergic to pain-killers, that's a miracle."

"Can people hypnotize themselves?" Jane Ewing asked.

"Excellent question. The answer is yes, yes,

and yes. In fact, that's my real interest in the subject: hypnosis as a self-help tool. I believe that with hypnosis, people can achieve complete mastery over themselves. They can learn to use their own powers to the fullest." He pointed at Jane and added, "You can do it too!"

Jane blushed.

McKenzie sat up even straighter. Could hypnosis help her understand her own powers? Her visions were sometimes very confusing. And once they started, she could never get them to stop—her nightmare images came and went with a startling violence. Could hypnosis help her feel more in control? She thought of all the times she had wanted to use her psychic powers but had been unable to summon them. What if hypnosis could put those powers at her fingertips?

"Think about it," he told them. "What kind of person do you want to be? Brave, funny, confident? Well, what if I told you that each one of you could *learn* to be all those things?"

Just then the bell rang, and Dr. Chaney quickly passed out a homework assignment. McKenzie stared at the clock in amazement. It was hard to believe a class could go by so fast.

"Earth to Mack, Earth to Mack," said a familiar voice in her ear. Lilicat was standing next to her desk, holding her books in front of her with both arms. "I'm sorry to have to be the one to tell you, but class is over."

McKenzie slowly got to her feet. A few girls had gathered around Dr. Chaney's desk, asking him questions. She desperately wanted to do the same.

"Okay, Mack," Lilicat said, pulling her toward the door. "Stop drooling."

"I want to ask him something."

"Sure. Like what's he doing Saturday night?" Lilicat headed for the door. "If you still want a lift home, don't take too long."

Dr. Chaney had finished answering the last student's question as McKenzie approached his desk. He snapped his briefcase shut. She cleared her throat. And then he turned and saw her. He looked at her with piercing dark blue eyes . . . and smiled.

"Yes?" he said.

McKenzie felt a tingling sensation. For a moment she couldn't remember what she wanted to ask him. "Uh . . . I had a question." He waited patiently. "Ah . . . I've always been really interested in—fascinated by, well, para-psychology and stuff and, well, I think—"

"You think you have ESP."

McKenzie felt herself blushing bright red. Did

he hear this all the time from teenage girls with schoolgirl crushes? She glanced around quickly to make sure no one was listening, but everyone had cleared out of the classroom.

"Well, no, I—"

"Oh, come on. You're a little bit psychic, right? You can tell me."

That was a secret, one she kept closely guarded. But she found herself stammering, "Yeah . . . how did you know that?"

He laughed. "I guess I have a little ESP too. Listen, if you *think* you have psychic powers, you probably do have some—at least a tiny bit. You've just got to learn to trust them."

McKenzie nodded hard—too hard. Relax, she told herself. But she found this man *so* appealing.

"What makes you think you have ESP?" he asked.

McKenzie took a deep breath. "Well, I don't want you to think I'm crazy or anything—"

"I won't."

"But since I was a little kid, I've been having these visions. And they just seem to turn out to be true. One time I even helped the police catch a murderer."

"That's very impressive." He was staring right at her. He *looked* impressed. McKenzie smiled, feeling herself blush again. What did a blush on top of a blush look like?

"You know," said the teacher, "I'm going to be running some experiments tonight at my lab—"

"You have a lab?"

"Mm-hm." He popped his briefcase back open and removed a black leather appointment book. He studied that day's entries. "If you have some free time and feel like dropping by, I could run some simple tests."

Free time? Was he kidding? "Sure!" she agreed. Then she realized she hadn't even asked him what kind of tests he had in mind. "Uh, what kind of tests?"

He laughed. "Nothing painful—basic visualization skills, mind reading, random drawing . . ."

The psychologist took a gold pen out of his jacket pocket and held it poised over his book. "How does eight o'clock sound?"

It sounded fantastic.

She wrote down the lab address and Dr. Chaney's directions for how to get there. Then he walked her to the door, reaching past her to turn off the light switch. "Uh, Dr. Chaney? There's one other thing?" Why was everything she said to this man coming out as a question?

"I've only told a few people about these, um, abilities of mine. I don't want anyone to think I'm crazy, you know, and—"

"Trust me," Dr. Chaney interrupted. He looked at her with those incredible eyes and squeezed her shoulder with a firm hand. "Your secret's safe."

Waving, he headed off down the hall, working his way through the throng of students who were milling around their lockers. McKenzie leaned back against the wall. When he touched her, she'd felt a rush of excitement unlike anything she'd ever experienced before.

chapter 4

It wasn't until she was running out into the parking lot to catch up with Lilicat that McKenzie finally remembered. She wasn't free tonight at all. She had a date to go to the movies with Aidan.

It was December—cold and terribly windy. Large, menacing ice patches dotted the pavement; all around the parking lot were sad-looking piles of sooty old snow. Lilicat was waiting in her mother's little red Volkswagen, her parka hood up, the car motor running.

"I'm so stupid," McKenzie said as she got in, her breath coming out in gray plumes. "I just made a date with Dr. Chaney and I'm supposed to go out with Aidan."

Her friend's jaw dropped. "You made a *date*?"

McKenzie laughed. "Not a *date* date, silly. I'm just going to go by his lab so he can run some tests."

Lilicat gave her a knowing look. "Just you and him alone in his lab, doing *experiments*? Give me a break!"

They were passing the gym, where a group of hooded wrestlers in sweat suits had just emerged for their daily laps around the lot. How did they run in this cold? Behind them, in street clothes, came a tall, good-looking senior with a Nikon camera slung over one shoulder of his blue down jacket.

"Stop!" McKenzie told Lilicat, rolling down her window. "Aidan!"

He looked up, startled. When he saw her, he grinned and walked over to the car.

"Don't tell me," McKenzie said. "You were taking some pictures of wrestling practice . . ."

Aidan slapped his forehead. "A mind reader."

McKenzie was features editor for the school's newspaper, the *Guardian*. Aidan took photos for the paper. He was supposed to look for general school action, but he almost always took photos of sports.

"Are we still on for tonight?" he asked.

McKenzie shook her head and smiled guiltily. "Sorry, I goofed. Our new psych teacher asked me to come by the lab tonight and—"

"Basically, what she's saying is, she'd rather work than go out with a dweeb like you," Lilicat chimed in.

Aidan grinned in at them. "I'll show you how to set your priorities." Suddenly he shot a freezing-cold hand through the open window and started tickling McKenzie. In fits of laughter, McKenzie scooted over toward Lilicat, trying to get out of the way.

"Stop!" she screamed helplessly.

"Not until you promise to go out with me another night instead."

"I promise! I promise!"

Aidan finally stopped. He took out the new appointment book he'd been carrying around lately in an attempt to organize himself.

"Can you believe this?" McKenzie joked to Lilicat. "My own boyfriend has to schedule me in!"

Aidan was thumbing through his calendar, murmuring, "Karate, the photo club, tutoring, drum lessons—"

"Think you can make it this year?" asked McKenzie sweetly.

"I'm not the one who's canceling," Aidan reminded her. Then he looked up sheepishly. "How's next Monday?"

Lilicat pulled into McKenzie's driveway. McKenzie looked up at the house and smiled. Even on a cold, gray day like this, it always gave her such a warm feeling to come home. Home was a rickety two-story Victorian, with a big wraparound porch. Blue, her old black cat, stared down through the white gauze curtains of her second-floor bedroom window.

"About tonight," Lilicat warned. "Remember. If he tells you it's time for swim practice, don't take off your clothes." She ducked as McKenzie playfully punched her shoulder and arm. "Call me right afterward," Lilicat demanded.

Coming in the front door, McKenzie was greeted by the familiar sounds of her brother watching TV in the den and her mom conducting her realty business on the kitchen phone. McKenzie wiped her boots on the doormat, dumped her backpack on the hall table, and called in a singsong into the den, "You left your bike out."

"Mind your own bus-i-ness," Jimmy sang back.

McKenzie headed for the kitchen.

"I know it's a little bigger than you had in mind," Joanne Gold was telling a customer, "but it's such a charming house that I thought you should take a look." She waved at her daughter and mouthed, "Hi, honey."

Though she had her father's stormy gray-green eyes, McKenzie was always told she looked just like her mother. Both were tall with auburn hair and a generous sprinkling of freckles. But her mom wore her hair short, despite all McKenzie's instructions.

McKenzie picked a Fig Newton out of the cookie jar. Blasting in from the den came the sound of cartoons. Mrs. Gold looked imploringly at McKenzie. Taking the hint, McKenzie strolled into the den and told Jimmy to lower the volume.

Her brother, age eight, lay sprawled on the rug, his face about three inches from the TV screen.

"Hey, not so close," McKenzie said.

"Give me a break," he answered, without moving. She pulled him back by his sneakers. "Hey!" he yelled, and immediately scooted back toward the TV. When she pulled him back again, he attacked. Or tried to. She pinned him on the floor and sat on him. That always made him furious. "MOM!" he screamed.

"Thanks for helping, McKenzie," her mother called sarcastically.

McKenzie let her brother go and started upstairs. She wanted to be alone now anyway. She wanted to think about Dr. Chaney.

Clothes and jewelry were strewn around the room; every drawer was open. She had to leave soon. But she couldn't find the right outfit. She was now wearing her black leather skirt and gold turtleneck. She stared at herself in the mirror, trying several "casual" poses.

Then she caught sight of Blue. He lay on her bed on top of a pile of discarded clothes, staring at her with yellow disapproving eyes. She laughed, shamefaced. What was she doing? She was acting as if this were a date!

She glanced at her desk clock. It was a quarter of eight. She was going to be late. Hurriedly she daubed on some pink lip gloss and clattered down the back steps to tell her dad where she was going. Monday was her mom's book club night, which was lucky. It was usually easier to get permission from her dad.

She heard a high-pitched grinding noise coming from the basement; McKenzie smiled at the sound. That was her father: by day, mild-mannered hardware store owner; by night, the mad artist.

Shelby Gold was jigsawing through a silvery metal sheet when McKenzie knocked on the open door to his workshop. She had to scream "DAD!" and wave her hands before he noticed. He turned off the saw, pushed his protective goggles up onto his forehead, and removed his earplugs.

"Okay, sweetheart." He smiled. "I'm all ears."

But when she told him about her plans, the smile changed to a frown. "That *does* sound interesting," he said thoughtfully. "You know, I'd be interested in watching you take those tests myself. I tell you what—I'll come along."

"Dad!" McKenzie wailed. "What a gross idea. I'd feel like a little kid going to the doctor or something."

"Well, I can at least drive you."

"I'll be fine, Dad. I promise. And I'll call you from the lab to let you know how it's all going."

He was still frowning. "That's a cool one," she said, admiring his latest abstract sculpture— and trying to change the subject.

Her father turned his attention to the large

conglomeration of jutting metal pieces on his worktable. He scratched his head. "It looks a little lopsided, don't you think?" He was replacing his earplugs as she hurried out the door.

The drive to Dr. Chaney's lab took about thirty minutes. His directions were exact. With her heater going full blast, she drove down Main Street, glancing at the gaudy Christmas decorations. Downtown Lakeville was deserted at this hour, except for the Pizza Town parking lot, which was filled with cars and bikes.

She turned onto the ramp to I-63, went past the mall exit, and got off at Tucker Avenue. She had never gotten off at this exit before, and she soon saw why.

She found herself driving down wide, dark, deserted streets past looming factories that, in the darkness, looked like prisons. She clutched the crumpled piece of notebook paper on which she had scrawled Dr. Chaney's instructions: Go through three lights, then left onto Ivy Lane.

DEAD END read the yellow sign as she turned onto Ivy Lane. There were office buildings here, but they were spaced very far apart.

Halfway down the street on the right, Dr. Chaney had said. McKenzie strained to see. Why weren't the streetlights working? Then she found it—a three-story gray modern office building. At first it seemed totally dark. Then, up on the second floor, she saw some dim lights burning.

McKenzie nervously fingered her crystal necklace and shivered. The office building gave her the creeps. And her mind was beginning to send out warning signals. Over the years, she had come to be familiar with these strange internal messages of hers. She had learned to trust her instincts.

But she was dying to find out more about Dr. Chaney's research and whatever he could teach her about parapsychology. Just be careful, she told herself.

A female voice buzzed her into the building and instructed her to come on up. The lobby was dark. Apparently whoever owned the building didn't believe in splurging on electricity after hours. In the darkness she spotted a list of offices next to the elevator—there he was, number 241, Dr. John Chaney, Ph.D. The words looked so official. She felt a little better.

Red safety fire lights were the only illumination in the second-floor hallway. She made her way in the dark past gray glass office doors—a dentist, an accountant, a graphic artist, a publisher. Then she heard a murmur of voices, a man's and a woman's. She looked around but didn't see where the voices could be coming from.

C'mon, Mack, don't let an empty hallway stop you.

Two more offices, and there was number 241, the first lit door. Dr. Chaney's name was stenciled onto the pebbly glass in black letters. Strange, she didn't hear the voices now.

She knocked but heard nothing.

She knocked once more. Again there was no answer. She reached for the doorknob; it turned easily in her hand. She opened the door and went in.

Inside she found a small, cluttered but ordinary-looking office. The computer on the desk was on; its cursor blinked like a green eye. "Dr. Chaney?" McKenzie called. No answer.

Then the door to an inner office opened and a woman in her mid-twenties appeared. She wore glasses and a white lab coat; she had a wild mop of bleached blond hair and probably was pretty when she wasn't looking so tired and grumpy.

"McKenzie?" the woman said. "You're late!"

"I know. Sorry."

The woman shook her head in annoyance. "Have a seat," she told her. Then she stuck her head back into the inner office and said wearily, "Your student is here."

She headed for her desk. "He'll be with you in a second." She picked up a huge stack of papers and rolled her desk chair over to the computer, sighing loudly.

Why had she been late? McKenzie berated herself. She sat, feeling small and a little scared—she hadn't expected the appointment to be so official, like a visit to a doctor or a therapist or something.

She glanced at Chaney's assistant, who was frowning at the data on her computer screen. She also hadn't expected there to be anyone else at the lab. The idea of this visit being some kind of a date came back to her, and she felt foolish all over again.

"What are you doing?" McKenzie asked the woman shyly.

"Brain surgery, what do you think?" the woman snapped sarcastically. "I'm entering some of the results from Dr. Chaney's experiment. Which isn't what I feel like doing right now, if you want to know the truth."

"I'm McKenzie Gold; nice to meet you."

The woman just looked at her. "Tamara," she said, and continued with her work.

McKenzie was about to ask more about the

experiment when Dr. Chaney's voice interrupted.

"McKenzie! I was beginning to think you
weren't coming." He wasn't wearing the jacket
and khakis he had worn in class. He had changed
into a baby-blue wool sweater and black cor-
duroy pants. He looked smashing in this outfit
as well. In fact, he was even better looking than
she remembered.

"No trouble finding the place, I hope."

"Well . . . I was a little scared coming over
here."

McKenzie glanced at Tamara, who was still
frowning at her monitor; she could tell she was
listening. Why did that embarrass her so much?

Dr. Chaney laughed. "I know. Sorry. But
until my next grant comes through, this is all I
can afford. The money for hypnosis research
isn't exactly falling out of the sky, if you know
what I mean. You wouldn't happen to have a
spare million dollars?" He grinned. "C'mon,"
he said, "I'll give you the grand tour."

He led her down a narrow hallway into a
small room that was filled with cubicles. There
was a pair of headphones in each booth, for
listening to hypnosis tapes, Dr. Chaney explained. White soundproof tiles covered the walls.

At the far end of the hall there was another door, but Dr. Chaney turned away from it.

"What's in there?" McKenzie asked.

"Oh, storage," he said casually. "It's way too messy to show you."

Dr. Chaney's private office was a small, plain room, hung with diplomas and degrees. Among them McKenzie saw a Ph.D. in psychology from Marlboro University and a state license to practice hypnotherapy.

Over the desk hung a framed photo of a tall, dark-haired woman on a bicycle, smiling and waving. McKenzie's face fell. "You're married?" she asked.

Dr. Chaney's face became tense. "Almost," he said. "But that was a long time ago. Have a seat."

She sat across from him in a plush black leather recliner. He was so tall. Even sitting, he towered over her. She was five foot six, but this chair made her feel puny. Could it have been set a little low on purpose?

"Let's start with some card reading," Dr. Chaney said, pulling a pack of oversize white cards out of his top desk drawer. "Ever seen these?"

McKenzie shook her head.

"Good." He held up the top card with its back facing her. "Can you visualize the shape on the other side?"

McKenzie stared at the white card, hoping she could somehow see through it. All she saw was white. She felt silly. Why had she ever bragged about being psychic?

"Don't push," Dr. Chaney coached. "Just say whatever comes to mind."

McKenzie felt herself blushing. How humiliating! "All I see is white." She sighed.

Dr. Chaney looked startled. He flipped the card over to show her. The other side was totally blank. "Not a bad start."

McKenzie grinned, and they both laughed. He held up another card. "The first thing that comes into your mind. . . ."

"I don't know. A square."

"What color?"

"Red?"

He held up the next card. Now?"

"A blue triangle?"

Something strange was happening. He was holding up the cards more quickly now. And it was as if the whites of the back of the cards had begun to fade. With each card she saw a colorful shape shining through—a green circle, a purple triangle. When he moved the cards, the colors danced in the air.

Dr. Chaney's expression was growing more and more intense. A few beads of sweat dotted his forehead.

"Wavy orange lines," McKenzie said as Dr. Chaney held up the last card in the pack. He put the card down slowly, staring at her. Then he handed her the deck.

"Take a look." He typed some figures into his desk calculator as she riffled through the deck. She had been right—or close—on a lot of them!

He whistled. "Sixty-seven percent," he said. "Do you realize how far above the level of chance that is?"

McKenzie shrugged as if to say, "It's nothing."

Dr. Chaney leaned back in his chair; his eyes never left her. "And you're telling me you've never been tested before?"

"Not since I was six."

"Incredible. Fantastic! I have never, and I mean never, seen this kind of psychic ability. You've really got a gift, you know that?"

McKenzie beamed. She felt a rush of warmth. What a feeling to have this man complimenting her!

He gave her more tests. He thought of a number between 1 and 20, and she had to guess what it was. She was able to guess correctly seven times out of ten. He turned his back and doodled images on pieces of paper. She drew random images as well. Again and again, her pictures roughly matched his.

"Listen," Dr. Chaney said after about forty-five minutes, "I'd be interested in testing you some more. Can you stick around?"

"Sure," McKenzie gushed. "You know, what I was kind of hoping was that I could find some way to control my visions. They sort of come and go when they please and—"

"Control," Dr. Chaney echoed, interrupting her. "That's really the name of the game, isn't it? I mean, wouldn't it be great to be in control of all the parts of your life, all the time?"

"Yeah . . ."

"McKenzie, this is going to sound like a lot of baloney, but believe me, I know. I've been through it all myself—and this hypnosis stuff really works. With your psychic ability? And my help? You can get control."

"Well, that'd be great."

They both laughed. "It will be great," he said confidently. "I mean, you'll learn to control your visions like *that*—" He snapped his fingers hard. Then he jumped up. "Have you ever been hypnotized?"

McKenzie thought of Robb in class, removing his shirt. "No," she said slowly.

Dr. Chaney laughed. "You're thinking of that stunt I pulled in class today, right?"

He was right. Who was the mind reader here?

"That was totally wrong of me," he went on. "I should never have done it. But he made me so mad, picking on that kid with the stutter. What's his name?"

"Paul."

"Paul, yes. Anyway, in the kind of hypnosis I'd do with you, you'd stay in control at all times. That's the whole point of what I do, in fact—it's to give you *more* control, not less. I hope you know you can trust me. Because that's important for the work."

"I—"

"I can't tell you how exciting this is. Do you know how rare you are? I mean, do you realize how much control you could have over your habits, your mind, your body, your feelings?"

He stopped, as if he had just remembered something. "How old are you?"

"Sixteen."

He looked disappointed. "Your school probably wouldn't appreciate it if they found out I was hypnotizing one of their students."

"Oh, I won't tell anyone."

He smiled. "Good. Our work should be private anyway. Just between us."

Something was bothering McKenzie. Something she had remembered, but then forgot. "I need to call my folks," she said, half rising. "I promised I would when I—"

He gently pushed her back into the chair and rolled it toward the other side of the office. "After," he said. "First, I want to see how hypnotizable you are."

He had rolled the chair out of the light. He looked down at her as if from a great height. "Look up," he said. "Try to roll your eyes all the way up, so that only the whites are showing."

"What?"

"I know it sounds strange, but trust me. It's one of the simple indicators of hypnotizability, showing your ability to focus."

McKenzie rolled up her eyes as instructed. It was hard for her to concentrate with Dr. Chaney standing so close.

"Oh, you can do better than that," he chided.

Her cheeks burned. She liked it a lot better when he complimented her. She redoubled her efforts, feeling her eyes roll up even farther. And then a little farther.

"And hold it," he said. She held the pose for a moment. This must look awfully attractive, she thought.

"Great," he said. "You can stop now." She blinked and looked up at him. He was grinning so broadly she almost gasped. "I would guess that you're in the top five percent of the scale. That means you're capable of the deepest trances."

"Is that good?"

"Good?" Dr. Chaney had moved away and was sliding a cassette into a pull-out stereo and tape deck. "McKenzie, this is so exciting! With your abilities," he shook his head in amazement, "I'll bet you can learn to exert tremendous power over yourself. You could even enhance your psychic abilities—not that you need to."

"I'd like to." Her voice was eager.

"Well, then we will! I mean, at the very least I'm sure we can help you gain control over them. It's a mind-boggling tool. You get good at this and you'll be able to change any part of your behavior in about a half a second. For instance, if you were overeating—"

He smiled at her, his eyes twinkling. "But I can see that's not one of your problems."

She flushed.

"Here," he said, "I'll show you. Do you have any phobias that bother you? Any silly fears that get in your way and hold you back?"

The rope in gym class swung before her eyes. She saw the kids below her. Felt the dizzying fall.

"Fear of crowds?" he suggested. "Fear of flying? Fear of tests? Anything like that?"

Go ahead and tell him, she thought. But her instincts told her to stop. She knew this strange feeling well. It was that bizarre warning system of hers. She held back.

Dr. Chaney looked at her knowingly. "Whatever it was you just decided not to say, tell me."

Again he had read her mind! "No," she said. "It's nothing, really—"

"I see you have one phobia we have to work on. Fear of hypnotists!" He laughed, and she couldn't help laughing too. "I know fear is an embarrassing emotion," he continued, "but it doesn't have to be. It's just a feeling like any other. You can tell me."

"Well," she said, "I do have this little fear of heights."

Dr. Chaney snapped his fingers and said, "It's gone. Just a few hypnosis sessions, and we can totally cure it."

She tried to get out of the chair, but he was blocking her way. "I don't know," she said. "It's getting kind of late. And I'd better call my parents."

"This will just take a minute. Besides, it's the only way we'll know if you're *really* hypnotizable."

"But I thought you said—?"

"The eye-roll test gives us an indication, but that's all. The only way to know for sure is to try the real thing." He expertly maneuvered the knobs on the recliner so that she tilted back to a more relaxing angle.

"Now gently clasp your hands together, like so. That's right, as if you were praying."

He put his hands on her hands—and she shivered. For an instant she thought of protesting, but then didn't. She was curious—she had to admit it. What would hypnosis feel like? She wanted to know. And his voice was so soothing.

"Study the way your fingers intertwine and wind together like rope. Now imagine your hands becoming stiff. In your mind, see them being glued together like two pieces of wood."

She felt another flash of warning. She wished she hadn't told him about her fear of heights. But now she was closing her eyes and starting to relax, and it was as if she were swirling down, down. She tried to fight it. She tried to focus on something else, something other than the feeling of her hands, welded together like two blocks of wood.

"Even if you wanted to move your fingers, you couldn't," he told her.

That's not true, she told herself. That's just make-believe. But her own voice was growing fainter and fainter, and the darkness behind her eyes was growing deeper. Her vision felt blurry. Soon she was totally in his power.

chapter 5

She was floating. Her body had shrunk to the size of a dust mote, and she was just drifting in space.

"Amazing," she heard Dr. Chaney say. "Do you know how deep you're going? On a first trance, this is stupendous."

She had no sense of time. How long had this been going on? A minute? An hour?

"Tell me about the last time you felt any fear of heights."

She didn't have to think back far. "Today. In gym."

"Tell me."

She told him what had happened. It made her shake all over again just thinking about it.

"Good. Now I want you to picture the same incident, only this time we're going to rewrite the script a little. Picture your fear as something very specific—a ticking clock, say. Hold that image in your mind. That's your fear. Now let it go. Just let it vanish. You threw it away. It's gone. Okay?"

"Okay."

"Good. Now picture yourself walking over to the rope again. Only this time you don't feel any fear, because you threw all your fear away. Understand?"

Soon, in her mind, she was climbing the rope easily, totally without fear. She did it over and over again.

She wasn't sure how he brought her out of the trance. She opened her eyes, focused: he was smiling at her warmly. "We're off to an excellent start. Did I say excellent? Magnificent!"

He pulled open a drawer and looked through several cassettes. He handed her one. "Listen to this as often as you can. Even while you're sleeping."

"What is it?"

"A subliminal tape. Sounds like plain music, but underneath is me, reinforcing those messages we just laid in. You can't hear it with your conscious mind, but your unconscious mind will hear it, and that's what counts.

"You can also start practicing putting yourself in a trance, using the same procedure we just did. Start by gently clasping your hands together. After a while that will become your key command."

"My what?"

"Key command. When you get hypnotized a lot, your brain begins to associate whatever physical gestures or induction words you use with the trance itself. So when you clasp your hands together, your brain remembers the whole procedure and you go right under."

Dr. Chaney crossed to his desk and retrieved his black appointment book. "Be here next Monday night—same time, same place, same channel. Okay?"

"Okay," she said. It was so hard to say no to him, or even maybe. He made a note and, still smiling, ushered her back into the main waiting room.

"Good night," she told Tamara, who was still typing away.

"Good night," Tamara answered brusquely. She stretched and yawned, then glanced darkly at Dr. Chaney. "How much longer are you planning on keeping me here, anyway?"

Dr. Chaney laughed. "Actually, Tamara," he said, "I've got a little more data for you to enter."

Tamara stared at him blankly. McKenzie waited for a sarcastic comeback, but none came. In fact, Tamara now smiled as if this were wonderful news. "Okay," she said sweetly, heading into Dr. Chaney's office.

"It's on my desk," he called after her. Then he walked McKenzie to the door. As he said good-bye, he put a hand on her shoulder.

When she got outside to her car, the spot he had touched still felt chilled to the bone.

"Far out! He said that?"

"And then he said he wanted to work with me again—like often."

"Oooh, I'll bet!"

As soon as she got home, McKenzie had pulled the hall phone into her room and called Lilicat.

"And did he try to hypnotize you too?" Lilicat asked.

"Well . . ." McKenzie stammered.

"He *did,* didn't he?"

"Lilicat!" McKenzie exclaimed. "You're not letting me talk."

It was going to be hard not telling her about the hypnosis session. But she had promised Chaney. And it felt cool to have a secret with him, something she didn't even tell her best friend.

Excited, she paced back and forth, holding the phone. "My parents were sort of mad when I got home. They made me promise to call next time I'm out late or I'll be grounded."

"So next time you'll call. I don't want to hear about your parents, Mack. Tell me about Dr. Chaney."

McKenzie hesitated. "There's one bad thing," she said. "Something bothers me about the guy."

"What?"

"I can't quite put my finger on it. But when I got there, I was feeling all this fear and—" She hesitated. "I get cold shivers whenever he touches me."

Lilicat laughed. "Sounds like a worse crush than I thought!"

"No, I'm serious. It's not a pleasant sensation. It's like I'm suddenly really, really cold."

"When do you see him again?"

"A week from to—" McKenzie stopped short. "I can't believe it. Oh, no! I couldn't have!"

chapter 6

"I've done it again. I just blew another date with Aidan," McKenzie told Lilicat. "Let me call you right back."

"You've got *another* appointment with the guy?" Aidan said. He sounded pretty annoyed.

"It's just that he's excited because he thinks I've got such amazing psychic talents. He wants to study me."

"Yeah, well, I'm not so sure I want some teacher studying you. I like to do all the studying myself."

"Aidan, it's nothing like that!" She was glad she had decided not to tell him about the hypnosis either. He was annoyed enough about the ESP experiments.

There was silence at the other end. Then Aidan seemed to switch gears. "All right," he said, "what time is the appointment?"

"Eight."

"Okay, so why don't we have dinner at least? I can pick you up around five and take you to Louie's for burgers. Or are you having dinner with him too?"

"Of course not." She tried to laugh off the sarcasm in Aidan's voice.

But when she hung up, she wasn't worrying about Aidan being angry. She was thinking about Dr. Chaney. Even later, as she nodded off to sleep, she was still picturing her teacher's piercing blue eyes.

chapter 7

The next afternoon, when McKenzie walked into Dr. Chaney's class, she found him sitting with his feet up on his desk and a pair of Jockey shorts on his head.

People were laughing, but he was keeping a straight face. When everyone had arrived, he began, "Today I'd like to say a few words about embarrassment."

That made everyone laugh some more.

"We all know what that's like, right?" Dr. Chaney went on. "Embarrassment is like—like having to wear your underwear on your head." He removed the shorts and began folding them into a ball. "But what if I told you that it was possible never to feel embarrassed again? How would *that*"—he tossed the underwear up in the air—"grab you?"

McKenzie turned to watch the trajectory of the falling white cloth. He had thrown the underwear right at Jane—she instinctively reached out and grabbed them. Then she blushed as the class now aimed its raucous laughter at her.

"Good catch," Dr. Chaney complimented. "But why are you blushing?"

Jane tossed the underwear back. He caught it. "Embarrassed?" he asked.

"No."

"Not even a little bit?"

"No."

"I need a volunteer for a demonstration, Jane. How about you?"

Jane shook her head. "Not me. I don't get embarrassed."

"Never? Never say never!"

He circled Jane's desk, walking behind her. You could see her trying to keep herself from turning and looking up at him to check on what he was doing.

"How about now?" He laid the underwear right on top of her head. Jane yanked the white cloth off her head fast, throwing it on the floor, and the class responded with catcalls and jeers.

Jane's cheeks now sported big red circles of blush like a china doll.

"Looks like you do get embarrassed," Dr. Chaney said. He put a hand on her shoulder. "But that's okay. We all do. Until we learn to control it. C'mon."

He led her to the front of the class for his demonstration. McKenzie looked at Dr. Chaney. His eyes shone with excitement.

Was she wrong? Or had Dr. Chaney just enjoyed embarrassing Jane? She forced herself to put the question out of her mind.

"What makes something embarrassing?" he asked the class. "I'll tell you the answer. It's all up here." He tapped his forehead. "Unless you *tell* yourself that something is embarrassing, it won't be embarrassing. It's that simple. It's a matter of where you put your focus. Okay, what I want you all to do right now is just stare at Jane and embarrass her. Jane, your task is even simpler—just let them look at you."

Still red-faced, Jane stared back at the class. But she was badly outnumbered. Twenty-four pairs of eyes bored in on her. And as the class stared she began to fidget, clasping her hands together, unclasping them, hiding them behind her back, shifting her balance to her left foot, her right. And all the time her face was getting redder and redder.

"Okay—cut!" Dr. Chaney draped a protective arm around Jane's shoulders. "How did she look?" he asked his students.

"Embarrassed!" the class shouted in unison.

He whispered something in Jane's ear. "Okay," he told the class, "start staring again."

But this time, Jane's blush disappeared. Everyone stared harder, but she gazed back calmly.

What was the secret? Dr. Chaney had told her to count the number of slats in the Venetian blinds that covered the windows in the back of the class. Putting her focus on the counting had removed any embarrassment.

"So for the rest of the class"—Dr. Chaney moved to the blackboard—"I'd like to focus on the power of . . ."

He placed the chalk on the board but didn't write anything. He held the chalk there, waiting; all eyes were on him. Then he wrote the word on the board:

F-O-C-U-S!

A tall blond girl stood somewhere way up high. She was on a stone platform. She held her arms stiffly at her sides. Her eyes were glazed. She looked like a sleepwalker.

She was preparing to dive. That was it. She was going to dive off the highest platform at the pool. But she was facing backward. She was going to do a back flip.

There was total silence. But people were there. Hundreds of them. The bleachers on both sides of the pool were packed. And everyone was staring upward. Staring at the diver who was about to dive into the pool.

But the pool. The pool!

Way down below, the pool was completely empty. Not a drop of water in sight. Just hard, pale blue cement.

McKenzie looked back at the girl. Her blond hair was clipped short. She wore a dark blue bathing suit with a white logo. Lakeville Senior High. McKenzie's own school.

Now she recognized the diver. It was Jane Ewing.

"Jane!" she cried. "Don't jump! There's no water in the pool!"

But Jane didn't even turn her head. Her eyes were closed now. She hadn't heard.

McKenzie realized she would have to climb up and warn her. And fast. She climbed higher, higher, screaming to Jane. But still Jane didn't respond. McKenzie looked down. She had gone way up, farther than she ever could have gone before. She must be cured of her fear of heights! But there was no time to think about that now. *"Jane!"* she screamed again. *"Don't jump!"*

But like a zombie, Jane ignored her warnings. She slowly tapped her foot on the stone. Three times. She bent her knees. Then she jumped.

"Noooooooo!" screamed McKenzie, sitting up in bed. She was breathing hard, her body slick with sweat.

Someone was knocking at her bedroom door. The door opened. It was her father. He flicked on the overhead light and ran to her. "It's okay, it's okay," he told her, stroking her damp hair. "You're having a nightmare."

McKenzie was gasping too hard to answer.

"You were yelling in your sleep," he said.

"What—was I saying?"

"Don't jump, don't jump," Shelby answered, frowning. He was wearing his blue pajamas, and what little hair he had on his head was all mussed. He looked worried. "Want to tell me about it?"

McKenzie looked around the room, confused to find herself at home, in her own room, and not at the pool. Blue was huddled in the corner, looking terrified.

"No," she said, "just a silly nightmare. What time is it?"

"Eleven thirty."

Eleven thirty. Wednesday night.

"Did I wake you up?"

"Don't worry about that."

"Sorry."

She dropped her hand over the side of the bed and wiggled her fingers at Blue, making his favorite *tss-tss* sound. Warily, he approached and let her pet him.

Her dad was still frowning. "I hope those bad dreams of yours aren't starting again."

"Oh, I'm sure they're not."

He waited a moment more, then patted her hand and moved toward the door. He paused by the light switch. "On or off?"

"Off."

"Sweet dreams this time, okay?" he said in the dark.

After the door closed, she shut her eyes. She opened them again right away. It was hard not to picture Jane, diving . . . the stone pool. She shuddered. It all seemed so real to her. Just a dream, she promised herself. But then she remembered the image of Jane hitting the floor of the pool and she sat bolt upright.

It wasn't a dream at all.

It was real.

chapter 8

"But I can do it!" Jane pouted, waving her hand angrily to help make her point.

Coach Andrews folded her arms tightly across her chest. She didn't answer—which apparently meant "No."

It was Thursday. Haunted by her nightmare from the night before, McKenzie had kept an eye on her friend the entire day. It was as if she had to keep checking to make sure Jane was really all right. She couldn't help it. Now she had stopped in to watch diving practice.

As Jane continued to argue McKenzie changed seats, moving closer to the pool's edge, trying to listen in.

"Jane," Ms. Andrews was saying, "an inward

two and a half? In the tuck position? You're just not ready."

"Hey," said Jane, a catch in her voice. "You're my coach. You're supposed to support me, encourage me, help me to get over my blocks. Not hold me back!"

Ms. Andrews reddened. "I'm also supposed to protect you. And until you're ready, that's a very dangerous dive."

"I'm ready. I know I am."

Ms. Andrews shook her head in disbelief. "What's gotten into you all of a sudden? I used to have to push you to do a half gainer. You used to be the most cautious diver on the—"

"Coach, I've changed, okay? I know I can do it. You said yourself if I'm going to ever be anything like Olympic material, I'm going to have to push myself to do more difficult dives."

McKenzie felt a sudden urge to stand up and say something. But she held herself back.

"Okay," Coach Andrews said, walking away. "Go on. But watch your form."

Now McKenzie did stand up. She made her way across the tiled floor to where her friend was doing some warmup stretches.

"So," McKenzie said with a sheepish grin. "You're going to try, like, a really dangerous dive?"

"Don't *you* start," Jane said in exasperation. "Aren't friends supposed to be supportive?" She flicked the bottom of her dark blue team swimsuit, adjusting it as she headed for the ladder.

Oh, God, thought McKenzie. Was her nightmare coming true? She stared at the pool. At least it was filled with water! Coach Andrews was sitting down now, looking worried, barking instructions as Jane climbed higher and higher.

And then Jane approached the edge of the incredibly high cement platform. Despite her session with Dr. Chaney, it made McKenzie a little dizzy just to look up at her. She felt an urge to cry out a warning but held it in.

Then Jane leaped.

Even though she didn't know much about diving, McKenzie could tell that Jane's dive was way off. It looked ungainly. She hit the water at an angle that came perilously close to a belly flop. Ms. Andrews covered her face with her hands.

But when Jane popped up out of the water, she was smiling and shouting in triumph. "See that? I can do it! I can do it! I can!"

Ms. Andrews didn't even smile.

The electronic music on Dr. Chaney's subliminal tape had a cool, driving beat. All week,

McKenzie had listened to it every chance she got. Now it was Monday, and she danced to it as she got ready for her dinner date with Aidan. The music shut out the sounds of the sleet that rattled against her window. She brushed her hair until it shone.

Just then she heard a loud yowling from outside her bedroom window.

She walked to the window and looked out. There was Blue. He was sitting on the icy edge of the porch roof, meowing his heart out in the freezing rain!

Blue was an old cat, something he himself seemed to forget. He was not always as agile as he needed to be to get out of the fixes he got into.

McKenzie opened the window. A blast of cold air hit her face. "Come here, Blue! Come on!"

But Blue just sat there, crying. He wouldn't come. Maybe he was stuck. She opened the window further, stuck her head out the window, and called again. Now the sleet lashed her face and arms. He didn't move.

She would have to go out on the roof to get him. It won't be so bad, she told herself. The slope of the porch roof isn't that steep. I'll just climb down there, grab him, and slip back in.

But first she had to get out the window. Blue

was still crying. She hoisted herself up onto the window sill.

Unbelievable—she was already beginning to feel dizzy. How was she going to climb down the porch roof? She couldn't even handle sitting still!

One leg at a time, she eased herself through the window and out onto the roof. Blue opened his mouth in a silent cry, staring at her as if to say, "Why don't you come get me?"

"Just a second," she muttered. "Let me prepare myself."

She looked down at her hands, which were clutching her pants legs. Prepare. Now was the time to try Chaney's technique, wasn't it? Maybe it really worked.

She gently clasped her hands together, interweaving the fingers. She stared at her hands closely, imagining that her fingers were glued together like pieces of wood.

Far out. She was feeling more relaxed. Her breathing was slowing down. Tentatively, she took one step forward. So far so good. Blue stared at her, meowing quietly now, but still not moving. She took another step.

It was as if her fear had just let go, floated away. She took another step, then another, and another. No problem.

But as she got close to Blue, the cat turned away from her. And jumped.

He landed safely a couple of feet away in the thin branches of the old willow that shaded the Gold house. Great, she thought, now he's stuck in the tree. McKenzie stood on the edge of the roof, eyeballing the distance between her and the nearest, finger-thin willow branches.

Not too bad, just a few feet. And she felt as if she were very light, as if she could float right over to the tree.

I have no fear, she told herself. No fear at all. She felt so strong, so calm. She knew she was high up, but it didn't matter. Nothing mattered. She wasn't afraid of heights. Why should she be? Gravity itself had ended. She was floating higher and higher. And she needed to save Blue.

She was crouched on the edge of the porch roof, ready to leap, when—

"McKenzie!"

Someone was yelling. But they were far away, far below. They didn't matter. Again she prepared to jump—

"McKENZIE!"

The voice sounded familiar, but she couldn't quite place it. She was above it all. She was free.

"McKENZIE!!!"

The voice was louder now. It was, she realized, Aidan's voice. She wanted to reach out and touch him. She opened her eyes. It was very hard for her to believe what she saw.

Aidan was way down on the ground—miles away, it seemed. He was staring up at her. He looked terrified.

She looked around her. Oh my God! It couldn't be true!

But it *was* true. She was standing with her arms outstretched, precariously balancing on the very edge of the porch roof.

chapter 9

She shrank back from the edge. All the strength had gone out of her legs. Kneeling on the cold shingles, she desperately looked for something to hold on to. What had she been thinking of? Had she gone totally insane?

She was freezing, she realized. And terrified. She was shaking all over.

By sheer force of will, she turned her head back toward the open window of her room. Not that far to go, she told herself. But she couldn't move an inch. It was too scary. She was frozen to the spot. And everything was spinning.

Now Aidan's face appeared, leaning out her bedroom window.

"Get back inside!" he yelled into the rain.

"Easy for you to say," she said through clenched teeth. "I can't move."

Aidan looked at her for a moment. Just a moment. Then he climbed out the window after her. He kept talking to her the whole time. "Walk up toward me," he was saying. "C'mon, you can do it. One step at a time. Mack! Walk toward me!"

Ever so slowly, McKenzie stood up again. She stretched her arms out wide for balance. Aidan was reaching out to her. "That's it," he said. "One step, Mack. One step at a time."

She took the step. But as she put her foot down, it didn't feel right. She glanced down. Which was just when her foot began to slip, and she realized that slick wet leaves dotted the icy porch roof. She had stepped on a patch of them. Now she was falling.

"MACK!" Aidan screamed, lunging for her.

But it was too late. She slid fast, slipping down along the sharply angled porch roof, toward the edge.

As she slid, she reached out and grabbed. But she couldn't hold on to the shingles. She went right over the edge.

She did manage to hook her fingers onto the metal gutter. She couldn't believe what was happening to her. Now she was hanging off the side of her own house!

White as a ghost, Aidan crawled to the edge and clapped his hands down on hers, holding her.

Crack! The old rusty gutter began to rip away from the roof.

Somewhere down below she could hear a boy yelling. Jimmy!

"Hold on!" screamed Aidan. Crouching down and bracing himself, he pulled back hard. The gutter gave way. McKenzie could feel it swing past her. But Aidan had her wrists in a viselike grip.

He was pulling with all his might. He jerked back, and she got about a foot of the way back on the roof. Kicking her legs wildly, she tried to shift her weight forward, but it was useless. Suddenly Aidan jerked backward again. Now she was able to swing one foot up onto the roof. He kept yanking hard until they both fell back onto the roof.

Then Aidan led her back in through her bedroom window. He closed the window behind her, locking it. They were safe. For a moment neither could speak. A frigid drop of rainwater ran down her cheek. She was freezing. She had begun to shake again. She hugged him, hard.

"Now," he said finally. "Would you mind telling me what you were doing?"

"I—I don't know. I—" McKenzie felt another rush of fear. She had been so close to falling. She was near tears. Don't cry, she told herself. Think, think! What happened?

"I heard Blue meowing," she said, moving away from Aidan as she tried to reconstruct the event. It was coming back to her now. . . . "Blue was on the roof. I went out to get him."

Aidan gave her a curious look. He pointed past her, out the window. On the ground, safely out of the willow tree, Blue was scurrying across the street. He ducked under a parked car.

But McKenzie was remembering now. Blue had jumped onto the tree. She had thought he was stuck there. And then she had just decided to go for it, to see if Dr. Chaney's technique really worked.

"You were acting like a zombie when I first got here," Aidan said.

McKenzie tried to laugh this off. "I was just concentrating real hard, that's all." She glanced out the window at the scene of the crime. "I was doing great until you started screaming. That's what threw me off."

"Oh, right. So now it's my fault you almost fell?"

She shook her head. "I'm sorry. Just kidding. Bad joke. Now, how about that burger you promised me?"

But at dinner, McKenzie was totally distracted by her memory of what had just happened. Aidan was right. She *had* acted like a zombie on the roof. She had been totally out of control. What did that mean? Had something gone wrong with the hypnosis? Had Dr. Chaney made a mistake? He had told her she would be in control. She shook her head. How could she have put herself in such terrible danger?

"The tickets are thirty-seven fifty each," Aidan was saying, beating time on the Formica table-top with his hand. "But I have all this lawn-mowing money saved up from the summer. And I know how you love Sting. So it's worth it, right?"

McKenzie nodded, but she couldn't help wondering again if she'd lost control of herself. She remembered everything Dr. Chaney had said to her while she was under. Didn't she? He had promised her she would. And nothing he said had seemed strange.

"So anyway," Aidan continued, "Boz'll probably want to double with us, but I'd rather it just be us two for once."

She wasn't listening. She kept picturing herself tightrope walking across her own roof.

"Also," Aidan said, "I bought you a Porsche and a huge condo and you're not listening to a single word I'm saying."

She tried to focus on him. "Sorry." She smiled.

He looked at her intently, then at her plate. "You haven't even touched your burger."

"I know. Listen—" She looked at her watch. It was seven thirty. "I'm just nervous about being late for my appointment. I think I better take off."

She had insisted on bringing her own car just for this reason—so she could make a quick getaway. She had to talk to Dr. Chaney right away. Something had gone wrong. She was sure of it.

Aidan looked worried. "I'll call you tonight," he said as she left, and she reached over to rumple his already tousled sandy hair.

Just like the week before, Dr. Chaney's office building looked closed and deserted. The dark hallways with the red safety lights scared her even more this time. Then she opened the door to number 241.

There was Tamara, typing at her computer, wearing her usual tired frown. McKenzie said hello, but got no response. She didn't have time to think about it, though. Now she was staring at the boy who was standing next to Tamara's desk, looking through a box of cassette tapes. He looked up at her and a big smile spread across his face.

"McKenzie! What are you doing here?"

She almost didn't recognize him, he was standing up so straight and had spoken so confidently. It was Paul Kelley, the stuttering boy from her class. Except—he hadn't stuttered!

"What am I doing here? That's just what I was going to ask you."

"Same thing you're doing here, I guess," he said, grinning. He held up some cassette tapes that he had picked out of the box. "Trying the magical world of hypnosis."

"I thought you didn't believe in it," she said.

"Oh, hey, that business with Robb changed my thinking. In a big way."

Listen to that! He wasn't stuttering at all. He was like a different kid.

"Here's the tape I was looking for," Dr. Chaney said, coming out of his office. He smiled when he saw McKenzie. "Be right with you." He led Paul away down the hall.

McKenzie took off her down parka, but there

was no place to hang it. The plastic coat hooks, which lined the near wall, were all being used.

"Looks like you've got a crowd tonight," she said to Tamara.

"Yeah—he's got a lot of subjects here listening to tapes. Which means more work for me, of course," Tamara said glumly.

"Subjects?"

"From the experiment."

"What experiment is that?"

"He calls it the F—"

A voice right behind McKenzie suddenly said, "I'm ready for you now." Startled, she whirled around. "Hey, easy," Dr. Chaney said. "It's only me."

"Oh! I was just asking Tamara about your experi—"

"Yes, yes," he cut her off. "This way."

As soon as he had closed the door to his office, she said, "Tamara was saying you're running some kind of experiment?"

He looked at her oddly. "Well, this *is* a lab, McKenzie. That's what I do. Research."

"About what?" she persisted.

"All kinds of things. Right now I'm trying to figure out what makes certain music relaxing so I can design better self-hypnosis tapes. Why?"

He was staring at her so intently. She worried once more that he might be reading her mind. Or trying to.

"Something really bad happened today. And I think it may be—" She wanted to say "your fault," but stopped herself.

He looked very concerned. "What?" he asked.

She told him about the roof, Blue, her trance, almost falling. He led her to a chair. He looked shocked. "Now listen to me," he said, "and listen very carefully. We're using hypnosis to try to conquer your fear of heights. That doesn't mean we want you to put yourself in danger. Ever. Understand?"

She felt confused and embarrassed. He seemed to really care about her, just like Aidan.

"You're going to have to use your common sense," he continued. "Always, always listen to the voice inside your head. That's the whole point—to make you trust yourself. Don't try to do anything to please *me*."

"Okay."

He took a deep breath. "Okay," he repeated, letting out the breath in a long sigh. "Thank God you're all right."

She was beginning to feel ashamed. Maybe she had been the one who messed up. After all,

Dr. Chaney wasn't the one who went out on the porch roof. She was.

Dr. Chaney had moved away from her; he was loading a cassette into the tape deck. "I was surprised to see Paul here," she told him.

"Yes, isn't that great? He asked me to help him with the stutter, and I think we really might—"

He stopped as the music began to play: gentle, New Age electronic sounds. "—Be able to cure him," he finished. He frowned. "Was he embarrassed to see you?"

"Not that I could tell, and he wasn't stuttering at all."

"Good. But maybe you shouldn't mention this to any of your classmates. From what he tells me, he gets teased mercilessly. We both know what it feels like to be teased, right? So I don't want him to feel like anyone has the secret of his new success."

"I won't say a word," she promised. She breathed a sigh of relief. That was awfully sensitive of Dr. Chaney. She was wrong to have thought so ill of him. She felt her trust returning.

"I haven't told anyone about *our* hypnosis, like I promised. Paul won't tell, will he?"

"Definitely not. C'mon, let's get started. Ready?"

She nodded.

"Good," he said. "Hands together."

That night she lay in bed in her long red T-shirt, listening to Dr. Chaney's tape through her headphones. She had planned to fall asleep to the tape. But something strange was happening.

She could tell that she wouldn't be falling asleep anytime soon. Her whole body was tingling. She knew what was coming.

Suddenly she saw her. Jane. On the diving platform. She leaped. The huge crowd gasped, rising in horror.

She took off the headphones and got out of bed. Why did this nightmare vision keep tormenting her?

She rustled around in her backpack until she found her mini tape recorder. She had bought it when she started working on the school paper, the *Guardian*. But it had also proved useful as a way of keeping track of these strange ideas and images of hers.

Sometimes when she dictated into the recorder, it helped diffuse her fears. "December thirteenth," she began. "A little after eleven. Just had the nightmare about Jane again. . . ."

By the time she had told all the details, she felt a little better. Maybe this time she would get off easy. No more scary thoughts. She clicked off the recorder.

And that was when it began. She started breathing heavily, blinking hard. Gasping, she arched her back. Images roared through her brain. The pictures rushed up from somewhere way down below, becoming huge, colorful closeups that made her cry out in terror.

Jane hitting the stone floor of the empty pool. The roar of the crowd. Jane's body, lifeless. The blood.

A siren screamed through her brain. There was Jane, unconscious, being strapped to a hospital stretcher. Her face was pure white, as white as the pillow under McKenzie's head.

The wheeling red light of the ambulance . . . emergency workers loading Jane into the back. Blood flowing from her head, her back, her shoulder, her arm. The doctors were hurrying. But from the way Jane looked, it was already too late.

chapter 10

"Jane!"

Jane lifted her head from the water fountain as McKenzie hurried down the hallway toward her. "I've got to talk to you for a second."

Jane wiped her mouth with the back of her hand and said, "Homeroom's starting. Want to walk over with me?"

"Sure. Listen, this will sound crazy, but I'm kind of worried about you."

"Huh?"

It *did* sound crazy, but McKenzie couldn't think of any other way to bring it up; she decided to plunge on. "In your diving practice you're being careful, aren't you?"

Jane ran her long fingers through her blond

hair and snorted. "What's gotten into you? You're worse than my mother lately!"

"It's just—you're not taking any extra risks or anything, right?"

They had reached the door to Jane's homeroom. Jane patted McKenzie on the shoulder. "I think you should seriously consider getting a life," Jane told her, and was gone.

"She's going to get stabbed in the back," Aidan whispered in McKenzie's ear as the scary music played louder. Wham! At the next moment, the killer attacked.

This was an annoying habit of Aidan's, announcing the next event in movies that he had already seen once or twice. McKenzie and Aidan had had more than one fight about it. But tonight she just smiled and whispered back, "Thanks. I don't want to get too scared."

It was Saturday night. She and Aidan were finally having their movie date, doubling with Lilicat and Jamie Hobbs. The movie was *Friday the 13th, Part IV*. Aidan's choice, not McKenzie's; she figured she had enough scary images in her head already. But since Aidan had put up with two broken dates, it was the least she could do.

Dr. Chaney had hypnotized her again on Friday. She hadn't yet noticed any ill effects.

When she told him she was having trouble sleeping (she didn't mention the nightmares), he gave her another, more relaxing subliminal tape. "Better than sleeping pills," he said. The tape had indeed calmed her down.

As they were strolling around after the movie, looking at all the Christmas decorations, Lilicat grabbed Jamie's arm. "I have got this intense craving—"

"Tell me," he said.

"For Uncle John's Coffee Heathbar Crunch."

"All right!" said McKenzie. Jamie looked incredulous. "Ice cream?" he said. "In December?"

But Lilicat was already pulling them across the mall parking lot in the direction of Uncle John's.

As they got closer they heard loud music. A bunch of high school kids had set up a boom box on the hood of a car. They looked familiar. McKenzie squinted. She spotted Robb Sterfeld and some other guys from the swim team. Standing up on top of the car, dancing to the music, was Jane.

"Hey, Mack," Jane called as they passed, "you being careful?" She laughed and yelled "Backward somersault!" With that, she flipped right off the car roof and just managed to land on her feet on the pavement below.

McKenzie yelped. But Jane only laughed. Robb yelled out his approval of the dive, then moved away from Jane and began fake boxing with one of his pals. The whole group seemed riled up and rowdy.

As McKenzie and her friends walked past them a car pulled up in front of Uncle John's. The driver was Paul Kelley.

"Heh-heh-heh-hey!" Robb shouted as Paul got out of the car. "Loo-loo-loo-look who's here!"

The other swimmers laughed and picked up the chant. McKenzie stopped, worried. Up ahead Aidan, Lilicat, and Jamie stopped too, waiting for her. Paul wasn't backing down and cowering the way he usually did. He was staring right back at Robb, a strange, blurry look in his eyes.

"There must be something in ch-ch-chlorine," he now told Robb, "that eats away people's brains. Because you certainly don't have any."

Robb looked surprised. Paul was the last person he had expected to take him on. Paul looked a little surprised himself.

"What's that you said?" Robb asked casually, moving slowly toward Paul.

Aidan walked over and tugged on Paul's arm. "C'mon," he said quietly. "Just ignore them."

Paul shook his arm free. He stared blankly at

Robb. "What's the matter?" he said. "Too stu-stupid to understand me the first time?"

Robb shoved Paul hard in the chest, pushing him backward several steps. Then Paul pushed right back.

McKenzie stood next to Aidan, amazed and appalled. Paul wasn't backing down. What had gotten into him? Robb was only about twice his size.

"You want to fight?" Paul demanded, poking Robb with his finger. "Let's fight it out once and for all!" His voice was high, but he wasn't stuttering. What was he thinking of?

Robb just laughed. Turning to his buddies, he said, "He wants to fight!"

When his head was turned, Paul charged, almost knocking Robb to the ground. Almost. Robb swung back into him, and Paul fell. He scrambled right back up.

"C'mon!" he yelled, motioning Robb toward him.

"Oh, please," Robb said, dismissing him with a wave.

"No. You've been picking on me all my life. Now *you're* going to find out what it's like." He started pushing Robb again.

Robb laughed, but he looked amazed. "What am I supposed to do with this guy?" he asked the crowd.

Just then Paul swung. He punched Robb right in the face.

Robb flew into motion. His first punch hit Paul on the side of the head, knocking the smaller boy sideways. Aidan dove between them, pulling Robb back. "Okay," he told him. "Enough!"

But Paul charged again, and his first punch caught Aidan flush on the jaw. Then Robb hit Paul so hard he stopped punching altogether. He covered his face with his hands as Robb hit him again and again.

Lilicat and McKenzie screamed at him to stop. So did Jane. But their voices were drowned out by the shouts from the swim team, cheering Robb on.

Aidan grabbed Robb's arms and pulled him away again. "I said that's enough!" he yelled at Robb. *"Enough!"*

McKenzie put her hand on Paul's shoulder. He was kneeling on the gravel, holding his nose. It was bleeding. He looked at the blood on his hand, then got up fast. He staggered away a few steps. He was by Robb's car now. On top of the car was an empty beer bottle. He grabbed it and raised his arm over his head.

"Paul!" McKenzie cried.

But it was too late. Paul smashed the bottle against the car. Now he was holding out the jagged edge. He rushed toward Robb. "Hey, Sterfeld!" he yelled. He lunged, but Robb sidestepped the blow.

Paul kept coming. He jabbed the jagged bottle right at Robb's face.

chapter 11

Robb ducked. Then he grabbed Paul's wrist. After that, there was no contest. He easily twisted the broken bottle out of the smaller boy's hand. He shoved Paul up against the car and began punching him mercilessly, landing blows to his face, head, and stomach. McKenzie covered her eyes.

When she looked back, Aidan was again trying to pull Robb off Paul. But Robb was in a fury. It took Aidan, Jamie, and two swimmers to wrestle him away.

"What got into Paul? That's what I want to know."

Aidan and McKenzie were parked in front of

her house. McKenzie was slumped all the way over next to the door.

"I mean, he's usually such a wimp. Suddenly, he's Joe Tiger." Aidan felt his sore jaw and chuckled.

"It's not funny," McKenzie said.

"Sorry."

Aidan had offered to drive Paul home, but Paul insisted he was fine, and hurried off by himself. "He wasn't badly hurt," Aidan reassured her. "Bloody noses look worse than they are."

She looked at him. He smiled. She smiled back. She wanted to tell him what was really on her mind. Paul's hypnosis sessions with Dr. Chancy. She thought of her own sessions. Her nightmare visions. She kept picturing Paul at Dr. Chaney's office. Dr. Chaney with his arm around Paul, leading him toward the back room. But she remembered her promise to her teacher. Pushing the thoughts from her mind, she scooted over in the seat and snuggled against Aidan. "You're great—a hero, almost. You know that?"

He pressed her to him. "I know." He kissed the top of her head.

She looked up at him and waited to be kissed. He didn't make her wait long. The kiss was warm and tender. She felt as if he were pouring good feelings back into her.

Headlights raked the windshield, and they instinctively broke apart. It was McKenzie's parents, home from their own trip to the movies. Her mom and dad both waved as her dad pulled their maroon station wagon into their driveway.

"Nothing like privacy, is there?" McKenzie smiled at Aidan.

"I've got an idea," he answered. "What do you say we drive out to the Cliffs?"

The Cliffs was Lakeville's main make-out and party spot. McKenzie wanted the privacy of parking at the Cliffs as much as Aidan did. But just the thought of going up there made her go cold all over.

"I'm not ready for that," she said. "It's way too high up."

Aidan shook his head. "Sure," he joked, "you can walk on the edge of your roof, but you can't park at the Cliffs." He didn't push her, though.

She got out of the car; so did he, slowly coming around to her side. She glanced back at her house—her parents were safely inside and out of sight.

Aidan was staring at her meaningfully, his blue eyes twinkling in the dark. "You didn't think I'd let you go without a good-night kiss, did you?"

He moved slowly toward her, and then his hands were on her shoulders, his mouth on hers. He pulled her up toward him. It was a long, deep kiss that felt so, so good.

She wrapped her arms around his neck, working her fingers through his long sandy hair. He pushed her back against the car, pressing hard against her. It was many minutes before they finally made themselves break apart and say good night.

As soon as she was inside the house, though, she started picturing Paul all over again. In the pitch-dark foyer, her back against the door, her thoughts overwhelmed her.

He had been so out of control. He could have killed someone, or been killed himself. Just like she had been out of control when she went after Blue on the roof. She could have been killed too.

And then there was Jane, acting so casual about her high dives. McKenzie shuddered. Somehow, some way, she knew Dr. Chaney was behind it all. And then, suddenly, she knew something else. She wasn't going to that lab ever again. She would tell Aidan and Lilicat what had been going on. Maybe she'd even talk it over with her dad.

She should have trusted her instincts right from the start. Those waves of fear she'd felt when she parked outside the lab. The cold shivers when Dr. Chaney put his hand on her shoulder. What was he doing to her? What was he doing to all his subjects?

She sat down on the chair under the hall mirror. Clasping her hands together hard, she tried to calm down. She stared at the way her fingers interlocked. Her breathing began to slow down; her vision blurred.

Then she got back up and reached into her father's overcoat, which was hanging on the coat tree by the door. She fished out the car keys, turned around, opened the door, and went back out.

What am I doing? she wondered. She moved down the driveway and unlocked the car. It was the strangest feeling, as if she were totally detached from herself. She could watch herself, like seeing someone in a dream.

Everything looked a little fuzzy. But it was real life. She was awake. Or was she?

"I'm getting into the car," she said to herself. "I'm driving somewhere. But where am I going?"

She already knew the answer. And she didn't like it one bit.

chapter 12

She was driving straight to Dr. Chaney's lab, as if she were on automatic pilot. "Maybe this isn't such a good idea," she told herself. But she kept driving.

The office building on Ivy Lane was as deserted and creepy-looking as ever. She stared up at Dr. Chaney's windows on the second floor. The shades were drawn, but lights were on.

Now that she was here, she felt fine. She saw the building in sharp focus. All fuzziness was gone. She was feeling like herself again. She couldn't help but wonder—had Dr. Chaney planted a suggestion in her head that brought her here?

All the more reason to confront him, she told herself as she got out of the car. She slammed the door behind her, as if to emphasize her decision, and headed inside. A man in a tan overcoat was coming out of the building as she went in. He held the inner door open for her and let her pass.

Halfway down the second-floor hall, she stopped. She stood in the dark, listening. Why did she always hear that murmur of voices on her way to the lab?

Something was coming over her. She always felt these cold waves on her way to Dr. Chaney's, but this one was worse than ever. Her teeth began to chatter violently. She put her hands on the wall, trying to calm herself down.

She found the door to office number 241 slightly ajar. She went in. The lobby was empty. For once, Tamara's computer was off. At first she thought no one was there. But the open door? Then she heard laughter coming from Dr. Chaney's private office. "Hello?" she called.

A moment later Tamara emerged from Dr. Chaney's room, wearing her usual uniform—a white lab coat and a frown. She looked surprised to see McKenzie—and not pleasantly so. "What are *you* doing here? Do you have an appointment?" was her greeting.

"Uh, no, but—something happened . . . and . . ."

Dr. Chaney appeared beside his assistant in the doorway, holding a stack of papers. "McKenzie!" He grinned at her, then he handed the stack to Tamara, saying, "Oh, Tamara, I have a little more data for you to enter."

Tamara stared at the huge stack for a moment, then looked up at him and smiled. "Sure thing," she said sweetly. She carried the pile to her desk, smiling at McKenzie on her way. That was strange, McKenzie thought. Didn't she hate me just a second ago? But McKenzie didn't have time to think about that now. She had to talk to Dr. Chaney. She was trembling all over.

"Paul was almost killed tonight," she managed to say once Dr. Chaney had led her into his office and shut the door.

"What!"

"Something's gone wrong with your hypnosis; I just know it!"

"Why don't you sit down?"

"He wasn't himself. He—he was crazy—he attacked Robb—I mean, it was like he was out of his mind or something, like he was just blindly following your orders and not—"

"Whoooa," Dr. Chaney cut her off, grabbing her shoulders. "Now, first, are you all right?"

She looked at him, startled, confused. "Yes, of course, but—"

"Is Paul okay? Do we need to call a doctor?"

"Yeah, he's okay, but—"

"Thank goodness!" He let go of her shoulders. "Now listen, you're obviously very upset."

"Uh-huh. I am."

"Well, if you're upset, I'm upset. And let me tell you something: I'm going to do whatever it takes to make this better. Okay?"

She couldn't help nodding.

"Okay. Now start from the beginning. What happened?"

She repeated the story. She was feeling much calmer. He was listening intently, and he seemed really concerned.

"There's something you've got to understand," he said when she finished. "Hypnosis just isn't *that* powerful. It's not going to turn anyone into anything. You're in control, remember?"

"Yes."

"Good. And besides, I've only been working with Paul on his stuttering, not on trying to convince him he's Arnold Schwarzenegger!"

"Dr. Chaney, please listen to me! I'm beginning to feel like I'm going crazy. Part of me didn't want to come here tonight. But it was like I was two separate people, and one part of me was going to come to see you no matter what. I can't explain it."

Dr. Chaney laughed out loud. "You wanted to come see me—that's not so strange. Last time I checked, I was a nice guy. Right?"

"Yes, but it was strange, I'm telling you. Look, Dr. Chaney, I just feel like this whole thing is getting out of hand. I want to stop the sessions."

Dr. Chaney put his arm around her; lifting her chin, he gazed at her with those dark flashing eyes. "McKenzie—what we're doing here is very important. You know that. We're on the verge of putting you in total control of your—"

"Total control? I'm totally frazzled. I'm quitting. That's my final decision."

Dr. Chaney sighed. He crossed to his desk. Then his glance fell on the framed wall photo of the tall, dark-haired woman, waving to him as she rode a bicycle.

"I'd like to tell you a little story," he said finally. "Remember I told you I was once almost married? Well, this woman—Mary—she was my fiancée. She and I were vacationing together at the shore. She was swimming off the docks, but the water was deeper than she thought. She panicked and started choking. At the time I was suffering from a terrible phobia—fear of water—and . . ." He trailed off. His eyes grew moist. "If it wasn't for that, I could have saved her."

Dr. Chaney wiped his eyes and pulled himself together. "Anyway, that's how I got started on this whole self-hypnosis business. So nothing like that will ever happen to me again, or to anyone else." He looked at her imploringly. "And that's why you can't quit. You can't. There's nothing more important than mastering your fears."

"But—" McKenzie began.

"No buts. Look, if you're feeling frazzled, hypnosis can help. Come this way."

"I don't know," McKenzie said hesitantly. "I really decided—"

But she was letting him lead her. And he was pushing her down, gently yet relentlessly pushing her into the soft, black, cushioned chair.

chapter 13

The waiting room for the school psychologist's office was decorated with posters of young rock musicians, athletes, and actors. Trying pretty hard to be hip, thought McKenzie.

She sat uncomfortably on the hard blue sofa, waiting. What could she tell this guy? That she had ESP and she thought her psych teacher was trying to brainwash her?

She laughed, something she hadn't done in a while. Maybe she *could* confide in the guy. She hadn't been able to tell anyone what was going on. It would feel great to tell someone, to talk about her trances, and to find out what Dr. Chaney might be doing to her. That was why she had made the appointment first thing Monday morning.

Wednesday was the first day the psychologist could fit her in. She figured there must be a lot of depressed kids in her school.

She looked up and caught the secretary staring at her. The secretary immediately looked away. She felt as if she could hear the secretary thinking, I wonder what's wrong with her?

"Nothing's wrong with me," McKenzie told her. "I just need some information." The woman looked startled. McKenzie could tell by her expression that she had guessed correctly.

Just then the secretary's desk intercom buzzed. "You can go in now, McKenzie."

McKenzie walked into the psychologist's office. Sitting behind the desk, smiling at her impishly, was a tall, extremely handsome man with gorgeous blue eyes: Dr. John Chaney.

"It's you!" she blurted out.

"Hi, McKenzie," Dr. Chaney said heartily. "I've been helping Dr. Karl, and when I saw your name in the appointment book, I volunteered to see you. I told Dr. Karl that since we've known each other for a while now, I'd take this session."

He was talking loud enough for the secretary

to hear. Now he smiled at the secretary as he closed the door.

McKenzie backed away from him. "Don't worry," he purred. "I'm a trained psychologist. I used to see patients full time. I can help you with anything that's botheri— McKenzie! Where are you going? Wait!"

McKenzie ran out of the office.

chapter 14

"McKenzie! Where are you going? McKenzie, come back here!"

She couldn't believe it—he was actually chasing her down the hall. Where *was* she going? Then she saw the open door to the principal's office. She darted in. Ms. Disney was on the phone, explaining to some parent how busy Mr. Pevny, the principal, was. McKenzie walked right past her.

"Wait just a moment," Ms. Disney said to the caller. "McKenzie, you can't go in there; he's got—"

But she had already opened the door. Mr. Pevny was in the middle of a meeting with a group of teachers. All heads turned toward her, surprised.

"Yes?" Mr. Pevny asked pointedly.

She tried to speak, but she felt like she might choke. With a whole roomful of teachers staring at her, shocked and annoyed, she couldn't do it. What could she say? "I—I—"

"McKenzie!" She turned around. Ms. Disney was staring at her, her mouth open. And in the doorway stood Dr. Chaney.

"Shut that door!" snapped Ms. Disney. She obeyed.

"McKenzie," Dr. Chaney said coolly, "I've been looking for you."

McKenzie's mind raced, looking for a way out. What am I going to do? she asked herself. She couldn't think of an answer.

"We are supposed to be meeting in my office." He smiled charmingly at old Ms. Disney, who blushed and smiled back. "Come along now," he told McKenzie.

With a hard grip on her shoulder, Dr. Chaney led her out. Get Ms. Disney to help you, McKenzie told herself.

But he was holding her so tightly, staring at her with such anger. What would he do to her if she tried to squirm free? She felt like a robot. She couldn't think straight.

He walked her back down the hall to the psychologist's office. "Everything's under control," he told the secretary, smiling. Then he guided McKenzie back into his office, shutting the door behind her.

"Sit down," he commanded. She sat.

But when she looked up at him, it wasn't anger that filled his face—it was concern.

"McKenzie, I'm very worried about you," he said. "You're obviously extremely upset."

"That's an understatement! I—"

"Well, that upsets me very much, McKenzie. Because I care a lot about you, and I don't want to see you upset—ever."

"Well, you've got a funny way of—"

"So let's talk about what we can do right now to make you feel better. What can I do to help you? You name it, I'll do it. Just tell me."

McKenzie's rapid breathing had begun to slow a little. She needed help so badly. Just the mention of the word had a calming effect on her. But he *couldn't* help her. He was the problem! "Nothing. Just let me go."

Dr. Chaney's expression of concern deepened further. "McKenzie? Don't you trust me? Don't you know by now that I would never ever do anything to harm you?"

She didn't answer.

"What have I ever done to harm you?" he pursued. "Name one single thing I've ever done that wasn't in your best interest."

She thought about it. It was true. He had never done anything to harm her. So why was she so scared of him? It suddenly seemed hard to remember why she'd thought she needed help in the first place.

"Look," he said gently. "Maybe we should start by trying to calm you down. What do you say? You've got yourself tied up in knots."

He snapped a tape into a cassette player—that lulling music. He advanced toward her. He began to murmur in that soothing voice of his, relaxing her into a trance.

McKenzie put her hand over her eyes, trying to block him out. I've got to stay awake, she told herself. But her body was feeling heavier every second.

". . . So I'm going to count backward from ten, and when I get to zero, you will be in a deep trance, okay?"

She wasn't sure if she nodded or not. But now she could hear him counting.

". . . Three . . . two . . . one . . . *zero*."

And then . . . then it was as if she had separated from her body again. As if she were watching herself from high above. There was

Dr. Chaney, leaning over her, pouring these thoughts into her ears. And all the time she sat totally still, her face a mask. From high above, she listened to every word he said.

". . . You won't remember anything that we say here . . ."

So he was trying to cover himself—and keep her from talking. Well, she could beat him at this game.

All she had to do was remember what he was telling her, right now.

Remember . . . remember . . .

But by then, her mind had gone blank.

And later she would have no memory of what he was telling her. Even though he said it over and over again.

chapter 15

McKenzie was the only one in the *Guardian* office. She was editing a feature story on the school's plans to renovate the library. Pretty boring. She tried to put in a few jokes to liven it up.

School had ended over an hour ago, and the building was eerily quiet. She was beginning to get a bad case of the creeps. She sure wished Aidan were there.

A familiar knock came at the door. There stood Aidan, Nikon camera hanging from his shoulder. "I'm here to see an editor of the school paper," he said. "I've got some sports photos she might be interested in."

She rushed into his arms. "Oh, Aidan, it's so great to see you." She hugged him hard.

"Hey," he said gently. "You saw me in the cafeteria just a few hours ago."

She let go and moved away, not meeting his questioning gaze. "You okay?" he asked.

"Fine, I'm fine; it's just—" She waved her hand at the empty room. "I get a little stir-crazy working in here all by myself."

She sat back down at her desk, and he came to stand beside her. He undid the clasp on the manilla envelope he was carrying and poured a pile of 5 × 7 glossy black-and-white photos onto the desk. "I think I've got some really good ones in here," he said. "If you don't mind my bragging."

McKenzie examined the photos one by one. There were shots of wrestling and diving practice. "Some of these look terrific," she told him. "Great action." He looked pleased.

"Listen," she went on, "there's something I've been meaning to talk to you about, and that is—that is—" She hesitated, then finished by saying, "This headache of mine."

Aidan smiled and began rubbing her neck.

What am I doing? she asked herself. Why didn't I tell him what I meant to tell him? Why don't I tell him what's been going on?

She was watching herself again. That same separation. Tell him, she commanded herself. But it was as if she had lost control of her own mind. As if someone else was giving the orders.

"How does that feel?" Aidan asked, massaging her shoulders.

"Fine. Oooh! Even better now."

"Well, I gotta go. The diving meet starts any minute now."

"Oh, please don't go!" Her sudden urgency surprised them both.

He looked at her, worried. "Why don't you come with me?"

She had recovered her composure. "That's a great idea. I'll just finish editing this one piece and then I'll meet you there."

He looked at her searchingly. She managed a smile.

"I'll be the guy with the camera," he joked as he left.

The door closed. She was alone again. She looked around the empty room. Suddenly she remembered something. It was the strangest feeling. She remembered something, but she didn't know *what*. All she had remembered was that she was *supposed* to remember something. She started to sweat.

It wasn't a good cleansing sweat, like when

you sweat during a long run. This was squirmy. Unpleasant. She felt it on her forehead, under her arms, on the palms of her hands, even on the soles of her feet.

Remember! she shrieked at herself. But it was no use. The glimmer had come and gone.

She stared at the phone on her desk. She could call Lilicat. Lilicat once joked that they were like each other's diaries, the way they talked every day. Well, today she sure had some important entries.

But she didn't move to pick up the receiver. And every time she told herself to call, she began to sweat even more. Finally she grabbed the phone and dialed with shaky hands.

"Hello?"

"Lilicat?"

"Hey, Mack! What's going on?"

Now, McKenzie thought. Tell her. Now!

"Are you there?" Lilicat asked.

"I'm here."

"At home?"

"No. The *Guardian.*"

"What's the matter?"

"That's a good question. That's exactly what I've been asking myself lately."

"Yeah? Just a second, I'm getting a bag of Fritos. Because I want to make myself nice and fat. Okay, I'm ready for you. What's going on?"

A drop of cold sweat ran down McKenzie's forehead and into her eye. She wiped at it furiously.

"Hello? What's the matter? You're scaring me."

"Trouble," McKenzie stammered. "Chaney."

She could hear Lilicat munching in her ear. "Chaney? What's the trouble with you and Chaney? Oh, no! McKenzie! You're not going out with him, are you? You're insane! He's about twenty years older than you are, for one thing. And Aidan—do you know how many girls are dying to go out with Aidan?"

"I'm *not* going out with Chaney!"

"Oh." She sounded disappointed. "So what's the problem?"

Tell her! McKenzie ordered herself. But she just couldn't do it. "Oh, I don't know," she said. "I'll talk to you about it some other time. I've got to get this article done."

"Okay. Sure. Just tease me and leave me hanging."

"I gotta go," she repeated. Then she watched herself do exactly what she didn't want to do. She watched herself hang up.

She held her head with both hands and stared

down at her desk. There were Aidan's photographs. One of the photos caught her eye. It was Jane Ewing. She was standing on the highest platform. Her arms pointed out straight in front of her, like a sleepwalker.

It was as if Aidan had photographed her nightmare. This was how it always began. She saw the empty pool, the dry stone waiting below. She saw Jane tapping her foot three times.

Then she looked back down at the photograph—and let out a scream.

Dark red blood was flowing out of the 5×7 glossy as if from an open wound.

chapter 16

The diving meet against Norwich High! Why hadn't she remembered? This must be the event she had been picturing. And it was about to happen for real. McKenzie tore out of the *Guardian* office. She had to stop Jane Ewing's dive before it was too late.

The Lakeville pool was in a separate dome-shaped building just down the road from the main school building. McKenzie hadn't stopped long enough to get her coat. She was running so fast, the icy wind hurt her lungs.

"DIVING NEXT FOR LAKEVILLE," boomed a microphone announcement as she ran up the stairs toward the pool bleachers. "JANE . . . EWING!"

The crowd roared. Gasping, McKenzie pulled open the doors and hurried inside. The place was packed with kids and parents. She had to push past several kids just to be able to see. Down by the pool McKenzie spotted Jane in her blue Lakeville suit, doing some last-minute warmup stretches. Standing nearby was Coach Andrews, her arms crossed, a stern expression on her face.

"EWING'S NEXT DIVE WILL BE A FORWARD DOUBLE SOMERSAULT IN A PIKE POSITION!"

McKenzie breathed a quick sigh of relief: this was Jane's usual competition dive, not nearly as dangerous as the dive she had tried earlier, the inward two and a half. But McKenzie was still anxious to see it. She pushed her way down the aisle toward the pool. Jane had started to climb the ladder.

Robb Sterfeld, McKenzie saw, was on his feet, hands cupped over his mouth, shouting his encouragement. She made her way toward him.

Jane was halfway up the ladder, past the first platform. She was going off the high platform.

All at once, the crowd fell silent. Jane had reached the top platform. And instead of preparing to do a forward dive, she walked to the edge of the board and turned around, her back to the water. McKenzie's heart pounded. Jane wasn't going to do a forward double somersault. She was going to do the inward two and a half!

"Robb," McKenzie whispered urgently. "We can't let her dive."

"Shut up!" he hissed. "This is a *very* dangerous dive she's doing."

"I know. That's just—"

"I mean, I can't believe she finally got the guts to try it. Her coach forbid it, but Jane's blowing her off. She's always trying to hold Jane back. Now shut up. If she gets distracted she could hit her head, easy."

"That's just the point!" exclaimed McKenzie.

Heads were turning. Coach Andrews paled and took a step forward. Up on the platform Jane stood at the edge of the board, composing herself. McKenzie tried to push past Robb to the aisle, but he grabbed her arm. He was holding her hard, hurting her.

And then she saw . . . across the pool . . . Dr. Chaney himself. He had just entered the room and was making his way through the audience and down the opposite aisle. As if he had felt her gaze, he now looked up. Their eyes locked. Those eyes, those magnetic eyes. McKenzie could barely pull her gaze away.

Up on the high platform, Jane seemed to be in a trance of concentration. She tapped the cement three times with her foot. It was all happening exactly as it had in McKenzie's dream!

Then it hit her. Tapping her foot three times. That was Jane's hypnotic key command. Just as Dr. Chaney had told McKenzie to clasp her hands together when she was afraid of heights. Jane was hypnotizing herself to override her own fears. Dr. Chaney must have taught her too. She must be part of his experiment!

Jane leaped. McKenzie opened her mouth to scream. It was as if everything had gone into slow motion: Jane, leaping high, gathering herself into a tightly tucked ball. Slowly somersaulting over—twice. And then straightening out as she went down past the stone platform.

Except she didn't quite get past it. First her head and then her left shoulder crashed against the cement. McKenzie's scream was lost in the crowd's sharp gasp of horror.

And then, utter silence. Jane was falling, in a mockery of a dive, her limbs all askew, down, down to the water below.

chapter 17

"Ewing?" The desk clerk checked his chart. "Room 616."

McKenzie had picked up Lilicat and then driven straight to the hospital. In silence, the two friends rode the elevator to the sixth floor.

The door to room 616 was partly closed, but McKenzie could hear voices inside. She pulled open the door and almost ran right into the man who was coming out—Dr. Chaney.

"McKenzie! Lilith!"

McKenzie didn't answer.

"Is she okay?" Lilicat asked him.

"Well . . ." he said. "No serious harm done. But I'm afraid she'll have to stay in the hospital for a few weeks—in traction. Her shoulder and back—"

"A few weeks!" said Lilicat. "She won't be home for Christmas—and she'll miss the state championships. She's been training for them all year."

Dr. Chaney frowned. "Yes, but the important thing, really, is that she's okay. And she is. A little groggy from the painkillers, but otherwise—"

McKenzie felt herself begin to tremble. Without meeting his gaze, she walked around Dr. Chaney and through the open doorway.

She hesitated a moment, trying to calm down. Then she turned the corner into the room. Sitting inside, looking ashen, were Jane's parents. Robb Sterfeld stood by Jane's bed. He didn't look very good himself. Jane was awake, but just barely; her head and shoulder were heavily bandaged. McKenzie wanted to ask her about the foot tapping, whether or not she'd worked with Dr. Chaney. But one glance told her she wasn't going to get any answers from Jane, not now.

"So then I started feeling like—" McKenzie looked at her hands. Her head was throbbing.

"Like what?" Aidan urged her on.

McKenzie, Aidan, and Lilicat were all sitting in Lilicat's room. She had told them a lot of the story already, but very haltingly. Every word was a struggle. "This is going to sound crazy," she said slowly, without looking up. "But I feel like he's here, listening, right now. Like . . . like I can never escape him."

She looked up. Her friends were staring at her strangely. Lilicat reached over and opened the door. "No one here," she assured her.

"It's just so hard to say no to the guy," McKenzie went on. "I feel like maybe he's brainwashing all of us—me, Paul, and Jane. I know it sounds paranoid, but I really think he's trying to hurt us. I just don't know why!"

Now Aidan stood up and started for the door. His face was dark with fury.

McKenzie grabbed his arm. "Where are you going?"

"To the principal. And then to the police."

"With what? I have no proof that Dr. Chaney had anything to do with Jane's accident."

"But he's hypnotizing you," Aidan said, "and telling you all these crazy things."

"That's the problem—and the scariest part. I don't remember what he tells me. I've only been able to remember that I tell myself to remember what he's saying. But that's about it."

Lilicat leaned forward in her chair. "If only there was some way we could listen in on one of your weekly hypnosis sessions," she said.

"There aren't going to be any more sessions," Aidan said firmly.

But McKenzie just stared at Lilicat. Listen in? The image that appeared in her head was of an empty dark hallway. Red lights. She felt cold all over.

"What is it?" Lilicat asked her, concerned.

She closed her eyes. Listen in, she told herself. She could hear voices. A low murmur of voices. She always heard them on her way to the lab. Then she had it. That part of the hall must be right outside Dr. Chaney's private office.

chapter 18

"Wow," whispered Lilicat. "Cree-*py!*"

With his lights off, Aidan parked in front of Dr. Chaney's office building. "Sure is," he agreed.

"Believe it or not," said McKenzie, "I'm glad you feel that way. It's nice to know I'm not the only one who gets the shakes at this place."

Aidan looked at his watch. "Ten to eight," he said.

"Okay," said McKenzie, unbuckling her seat belt. "Let's go."

It was Tuesday night during Christmas break. McKenzie had called Dr. Chaney earlier that day to tell him that she was having bad night-mares about her fear of heights. He suggested a hypnosis session, as she knew he would. He scheduled her for her usual eight o'clock slot.

Who knew what he was planning to tell her in this session! But this time—this time, Aidan would be listening in from the hall. And Lilicat would be keeping a lookout in the car, ready to honk and warn Aidan if she saw anyone coming.

McKenzie walked into the lobby with Aidan right behind her. Then she stopped short and pointed. The security camera. Tamara would see who was there when she buzzed them in. Aidan nodded and backed out of the lobby. McKenzie rang and waved at the camera. The door buzzed open and she walked through.

She didn't let the door close all the way. When the buzzer had stopped, she depressed the metal button inside the door so that it wouldn't lock. She let it swing shut. Aidan hurried in after her.

They made their way down the second-floor hallway to the first bend. McKenzie stopped, her hand on Aidan's arm. She could hear a voice. She pressed her ear up to the wall.

"I've got an appointment coming," Dr. Chaney's faint voice was saying, "but we can talk till she comes."

Aidan had his ear to the wall too. His face glowed red in the security lights. She nodded her head at him hopefully; he nodded back. He could hear.

She wanted to keep listening, but Aidan would do that, and tell her later what was said. She squeezed his arm and headed on toward number 241. Her heart was pounding so hard she felt as if it were trying to escape from her chest.

She knocked. No answer. She went in.

"All right, I've gotta go," Dr. Chaney said, hanging up the phone in his inner office. He smiled out at her. "Right on time,"

"Well," McKenzie said, "I'm eager to get to work."

"That's great," he said. But he was looking at her closely. Did he suspect something? She nervously wiped at her forehead with the back of her hand. What if she started to sweat?

"You know what?" he said. "This time let's use the back room. I'll get you started, but then I want you to listen to some more subliminal tapes. They really do a tremendous job, and—"

"Oh, I don't know," McKenzie said, flustered.

"What?"

"I guess I just feel so used to your office. I don't think I could go into a deep trance without sitting in that black chair."

Dr. Chaney was smiling at her strangely. His

eyes flashed. "Well, eventually we're going to have to wean you from my office so you can hypnotize yourself anywhere. But I suppose there's no rush. Come on."

As she walked in, she couldn't help glancing at the far wall. Just beyond that wall . . . She rolled the black chair closer to it. When she looked up, Dr. Chaney was staring straight at her. He didn't smile.

"Have a seat," he said.

She sat. This time, she was determined to fight him. She wouldn't let him control her mind. She would use her own powers to stay awake—and aware.

"I really need this!" she said loudly. "I've been listening to the tapes and doing what you told me, but the other night I dreamed I was standing on top of a skyscraper—"

Dr. Chaney was walking toward her. "Why are you talking so loudly?" he asked her.

He knows! She wiped at her forehead again. This time it was cold and wet. Calm down!

"Close your eyes," Dr. Chaney said. "I want you to try a new induction method today. I want you to begin by focusing on your own breathing. Try to picture your own lungs."

That wasn't hard. McKenzie's chest was heaving.

"Can you see them? Good. Now try to breathe using only the lower third of each lung. See how that feels."

As he led her through the focusing exercise, she felt her breathing slow down. In a few minutes she had to concentrate with all her might just to feel her lungs move at all, her breathing had become so shallow. Stay present, she told herself quietly. Use your powers. Now.

"I want you to imagine that you're holding a balloon," said Dr. Chaney, "and inside this balloon are all your troubles, all your worries. Really feel the worries inside that balloon. Then open your fingers and let that balloon, and your troubles, simply float away. Float away. Float away. . . ."

Float away. She was beginning to feel as if she were floating herself. Everything was growing dark and quiet. He was lulling her deeper into the trance. Think, she told herself. He's gaining control. Get away! Get away!

She imagined herself walking out of the office, right through the wall to talk to Aidan. But she couldn't picture Aidan's face. She could only see Dr. Chaney's—smiling and concerned.

In her mind she tried to wrench herself away, to picture someone else—anyone—instead. Her father. She pictured him at the hardware store, behind the counter. He had his back to her. He turned. The face was Dr. Chaney's.

And she could still hear Dr. Chaney's voice. It was very faint now, but she could still hear it. "You're not listening," he was saying. "Don't you hear what I'm saying? I know you do."

She was coming back to him. Despite all her warnings to herself to stay away, she was coming back into that office. The man with the burning eyes was getting larger, larger. She needed something to shake herself up.

She tried to picture Jane's accident. But she couldn't. Great! The one time I want the image . . .

"Maybe you'd be more comfortable in the other room."

No! Look at him, she told herself. Look at him as he really is. And she imagined Dr. Chaney removing a mask that was his own face and underneath . . . a wolfman with bloody fangs closed in on her own face. She screamed, but no sound came out.

"What are you so scared of? You've got to trust me, McKenzie. I'm on your side."

No, you're not! she screamed silently. But she couldn't help following him. They were going somewhere. She was following him. A new room. She was in a new room. It was all so blurry. She could make out only fuzzy shapes.

"Okay, I want you to imagine that you are lying on a warm beach, getting the massage of your life," the lulling voice continued. "Feel those skillful hands working over each part of your body. Feel them massaging your feet. . . ."

It felt so good! Then someone put headphones over her ears. She heard the sound of waves. She could *see* the waves. She was on the beach. She could smell the salt air. Voices spoke to her, right into her ears. "From now on," a voice told her, "you won't remember a word I tell you. Do you understand?"

"Yes."

She had spoken. She could see the letters come out of her mouth. They separated, danced in front of her eyes, and then formed back into words. They flashed before her eyes—"YES" "YES" "YES" "YES."

The man's voice was still whispering instructions into her ears, soothing words that felt like soft warm water as they floated inside her brain. And then . . . then she was falling. But it wasn't scary. It was pleasant. Everyone should try this. Head over heels. Down, down, down into the darkness that waited below.

chapter 19

McKenzie heard a loud click. She opened her eyes. She looked around.

She was sitting at a booth in the listening room. She wore a pair of large, helmetlike headphones, but the only sound was static. She took them off. The other booths were all empty.

Dr. Chaney appeared in the doorway, smiling. "All done?"

"What am I doing in here?"

"You weren't comfortable in my office after all," he explained smoothly, "so I moved you."

Obviously he was suspicious, but had he discovered Aidan? She stood up. She felt a little shaky on her feet.

"Easy now," he said, reaching out to steady her. "You've been in a very deep trance. Your deepest yet. Don't rush it."

Her deepest yet. She couldn't remember a thing. What had he done to her? She prayed that Aidan had been able to hear something significant before Dr. Chaney led her here. Dr. Chaney seemed to be in such a good mood. And that worried her.

"I've got to get going," she said. "My parents freak if I get home too late."

"I'm just leaving myself," Dr. Chaney said. "I'll walk you out."

Aidan, she worried. Is he still out there? "Oh, that's okay," she said, stepping past him. "I don't want to hang you up. I've got to go this second." She glanced at her watch. It was only eight thirty. It felt like she had been away for days.

Dr. Chaney was following right behind her. He pulled his wool overcoat off its closet hanger. "I'm ready." He grinned and flicked off the light switch. "I'm just going out for a bite to eat. I've got to be back around ten for a late appointment."

Dr. Chaney locked the front door behind them. "Boy, that was some session!" she said loudly, jangling the keys in her pocket and starting to whistle as they approached the bend in the hallway. Please don't be standing there!

They turned the corner. No one was there.

Then another terrifying thought rocked her. When they came out of the building, Lilicat would be sitting in the car. And Aidan too! Dr. Chaney would see them.

But as they came out of the building, McKenzie saw that her car was empty. At first she was relieved, but panic soon set in. Where had they gone? Were they all right?

Dr. Chaney opened the door to his dark green Jaguar. He looked at her as she stood there, confused. "You need a lift?" he asked.

"No, I've got my car."

"Okay, then. See you in class." He flashed his best smile and got into his car.

McKenzie got into her car as well. She strapped on the seat belt and turned on the ignition. Dr. Chaney revved his engine, then swung out sharply, pulling out past her. He waved good-bye. She forced herself to wave back.

It was only after his car had turned left onto Ivy Lane that McKenzie said, "Well?"

Aidan and Lilicat slowly unbent from their cramped positions, crouched down out of sight in the backseat.

"Did he see us?" Lilicat asked.

"No. Aidan, what happened?"

"I only heard the first part of the session. It didn't sound like Chaney was up to anything strange. But then he started saying he thought you'd be more comfortable somewhere else. I couldn't hear anything. So I went around to the front door. It was locked. I tried to jimmy it open, but I didn't get anywhere. Then I heard you guys coming out, so I ran back to the car. Where did he take you?"

"To the listening room—which is sound-proof."

"So we're back where we started," said Lilicat.

McKenzie pulled out of the parking lot. She didn't want to hang around here any longer than she had to.

"Do you remember any of your session?" asked Aidan.

"Not really. I was under pretty deep."

"That does it," said Aidan. "I'm going to the principal."

"But Aidan, I *volunteered* for this experiment, remember? If I accuse him, I better have the evidence. Otherwise he'll get off, and who knows what he'll do to me."

"I don't want you coming near this place ever again. You've got to promise me."

"I promise."

"Promise," he repeated.

"What are you trying to do?" She laughed. "Hypnotize me? I said I promise."

But she planned to break her promise that very night.

chapter 20

As soon as she had dropped off Lilicat and Aidan, McKenzie drove straight back to Ivy Lane. I don't want to do this, she told herself. I really don't. But at least this time she knew why she was going. There was something she needed to get.

Dr. Chaney's car was not in the parking lot—he hadn't come back yet. The building was totally dark. She looked up at the second floor. The shades were up, the windows black.

She walked into the dark lobby, glancing up at the security camera. There was no one upstairs to see her. Still, it unnerved her to see the camera's glass eye staring down. She tried the lobby door. It was still unlocked. She was in!

McKenzie took the elevator to the second floor. She walked down the hallway, around the bend. She slowed down. She didn't feel any cold shivers this time. And she didn't hear any voices. The lab, she felt sure, was empty.

She was starting to get nervous, though. This building was so bizarre! It was even scarier coming to the lab when no one was there. Especially when she knew what she was about to do.

She came to number 241. She tried to peer through the gray pebbled glass. She knocked several times. "Dr. Chaney?" she called. It was scary to hear her voice in the dark, empty hall.

Now she reached for the doorknob. It turned, but the door wouldn't open. It was securely locked. Aidan himself had been unable to jimmy it. That didn't mean it wasn't worth a try. She took out her wallet. What did they always use in the movies? A credit card.

Lucky thing she had one. Her father had gotten an extra American Express card for her— just for emergencies. She had never used it before. And this wasn't exactly the way her father had meant for her to use it. But it *was* an emergency!

She slid the credit card down the crack between the door and the wall. She fiddled with the knob. But she couldn't get the latch to click open. She didn't seem to be accomplishing anything with the card. Except ruining it. She tried a few more times, then put the card back in her wallet.

Now what? She looked down the hall. And that was when she heard—footsteps. She froze, listening hard.

But no. There was no one. She was just imagining things.

Imagining things . . . She looked back at the doorknob. What if she tried to *imagine* it opening?

McKenzie's powers had never done anything remotely like this before—making an object move just by sheer willpower. Telekinesis it was called; she had read about it once in a library book on parapsychology. But she had never even thought to try it. It seemed silly, trying to make something move just by thinking about it.

But then again, she was standing in a dark, scary hallway outside a locked office door. A door she desperately needed to open. Silly or not, what did she have to lose by trying?

So in her mind's eye, she pictured the lock opening.

Except she couldn't picture it. Not at all.

She tried again. Staring hard at the lock, she

tried to imagine the lock's inner workings. She let her vision blur. Her head began to throb with the effort.

And then—she saw it. She could actually picture the brass latch of the lock pulling out of the wooden slot in the doorframe.

She focused again and stared at the door. The imaginary lock had opened. But the real lock appeared to be as shut as ever.

She reached for the doorknob and turned it.

For a moment she just stood there, her hand on the knob, the latch turned all the way to the right.

Then reality hit her. It had worked. The door was open. She was in!

Inside, there was just enough moonlight coming through the windows to light her way. Feeling incredibly powerful now, she confidently turned on Tamara's computer. After it had booted up, the flashing message read: ENTER SECURITY PASSWORD, PLEASE.

So much for my new powers, she thought. She had no idea how to figure out the password.

There was space for only four letters. What could the password be? JOHN? She typed it in and hit return.

INVALID PASSWORD, read the message, USER TERMINATED.

The screen went blank. This was pointless, she thought. She'd never guess the password. But somewhere they must keep a hard copy of all the data Tamara was always entering. She turned the computer back off and squinted around the room.

No file drawers were visible anywhere. Where could they be?

She peered into Dr. Chaney's office. There, in the darkness, loomed the plush black recliner. She shuddered. But she couldn't see any file drawers.

She started down the hallway. It was darker here. No windows. She groped her way into the listening room. She felt along the walls. No file drawers here. So where?

She was about to return to the main room when it caught her eye. Farther down the hall, the one final door.

Too messy to show you, he had said on that first night. Storage, he had said.

She tried the knob. And it turned. But when she opened the door, she faced even deeper darkness. She couldn't make out so much as a glimmer. She inched forward, feeling along the wall for a light switch.

Her hand suddenly halted. She had heard something scurrying inside the room. She felt a rush of fear and just managed to keep from bolting. There! There it was again.

Holding the door open with her foot, she reached farther into the room, sweeping her hand along the wall. Her hand closed around something—but not a light switch. She felt it. What was it? A metal hook? Some kind of a box?

She pulled the box into the shadowy light of the hall.

It wasn't a box. It was a cage—a cage filled with rats!

McKenzie let out a scream and dropped the cage. It crashed onto the floor and popped open. Rats were everywhere!

chapter 21

There were two rats on her left shoe! Screaming, she kicked her leg violently. She succeeded in flinging one rat off, sending it flying with a sickening thud into the wall.

The other rat raced up her leg.

She smacked at it with her open hand as hard as she could, painfully stubbing a finger into her thigh. The rat fell to the floor. But the sensation of its fur against her palm lingered. She could still feel it after all the escaped rats had scampered out of sight.

McKenzie longed to do the same. Just run— run for her life. But the thing was, she had found them. The files. With her eyes better adjusted to the darkness, she could now see the file cabinets at the other end of the room.

The room, she could also see, was filled with more rat cages. Well, at least they were lab rats. White, red-eyed, tame lab rats. Who wouldn't bite her. But she felt like puking anyway.

She hauled over a chair from the listening room and used it to prop open the storage room door. Then she began walking, one step at a time, toward the files. She could see the beady red eyes of the rats in their cages all around the room. They were watching her. Where were those rats that got loose?

She was almost there.

Then she felt something brush lightly against her face. She jerked her head up, flailing furiously as she backed into the files. What was that!

Then she realized that what had touched her had felt like a string. She swam her hands through the darkness above where she had been standing, found the string, and pulled it. The light snapped on.

Lit, the storage room did not look scary at all. She took several deep breaths, trying to calm herself down. The rats in their cages now looked harmless, even cute. She turned back to the files.

She studied the labels on the file drawers: budget, phone, tax, office, employees. Not what she was looking for. Then she saw it. The neatly typed label read EXPERIMENTAL DATA.

Now she was getting somewhere. She pulled open the drawer and started riffling through. She pulled out several files labeled MUSIC EXPERIMENT. Then she stopped abruptly.

The next files were labeled FEAR EXPERIMENT. Fear! Maybe that was the four-letter password for the computer.

She felt as if she was in the middle of a fear experiment of her own. She breathed deeply again and again. Then she opened the file labeled GRANT PROPOSAL.

"Purpose," she read. "The purpose of the experiment is to see whether, through hypnosis, subjects can be helped to overcome their phobias."

Nothing wrong with that. She put the proposal back, leaned deeper into the file drawer. She pulled out a folder labeled CORRESPONDENCE. Inside were carbon copies of Dr. Chaney's letters to a colleague called Dr. Friml, whose office was in Houston.

"Dear Hermann," the first letter began. "Thank you so much for your note of encouragement. It helped me out of a terrible depression."

So Dr. Chaney got depressed? That was news.

"Well, it's official—Marlboro University has forced me to resign, all because of the incident with Mary."

Budget cutbacks, Dr. Chaney had said.

By the time McKenzie finished the next paragraph, she was shaking:

"The fact is, Mary *was* part of my fear experiment; I was trying to cure her of her water phobia. But there is zero evidence that she jumped into the water. I'm totally sure—as sure as I've ever been about anything—that she just slipped. It's no less horrible to me, of course, but to say that it was my fault is painfully insulting. My grief at her death is terrible. To be blamed for that loss, by anyone, is simply unbearable to me.

"Money is running low. This semester I had to teach a class at a pathetic local high school. In fact, if I don't get the Stine grant, I'm sunk. But I'm not afraid, I promise you. You cured me of that problem once and for all. I'm in control.

"In fact, I'm feeling incredibly excited and confident these days. In the past my proposals have all been turned down because of insufficient proof that hypnosis itself was responsible for the achieved cures. Now I have my proof.

Not only have my subjects overcome their phobias, they've achieved a total fear override.

"Many of my formerly phobia-stricken patients have broken through their fears so completely that they are performing daredevil stunts, stunts that even brave people would shrink from!"

She felt a surge of coldness flow through her. Daredevil stunts? Like her roof walk? Like Jane's dive? She read on:

"Of course, there is a danger involved in experiments such as these, especially when the experiment is so successful! Making sure that patients don't become too fearless is one of the things I'll have to work on.

"I'm afraid one boy seems to have completely lost control. But I truly believe this is a small price to pay, compared with the positive results, and the eventual benefit to mankind."

A boy who had lost control? An image danced before McKenzie's eyes: A boy brandishing a broken beer bottle in the parking lot. Paul!

She dropped the file to the floor, reached deeper into the drawer, and grabbed several more. The label on the next file made her stop short. A tingle of fear raced through her body. The file had her name on it.

And next to that was a file for—Jane Ewing!

So she was right! He was hypnotizing her as well.

"And what do you think you're doing?"

McKenzie's head jerked up. Standing in the doorway, wearing a heavy black coat, was Tamara.

"I was—I'm—" McKenzie fumbled for an excuse. But it was no use. She'd been caught red-handed.

Tamara began moving toward her. What was she going to do?

McKenzie decided not to wait to find out. As Tamara approached, McKenzie picked up an armful of the files she had removed from the drawer and bolted for the door.

"Hey! Wait!"

Tamara was chasing her. McKenzie ran down the hallway. She was in the main room now, and running, when *Wham!* She banged her knee on a desk. Down she went. The files scattered everywhere.

She tried to get to her feet, but Tamara was on her. She was trying to pin McKenzie's arms behind her back.

"Get off me!" McKenzie screamed, twisting away. Tamara was bigger, but McKenzie managed to push her off. She struggled to her feet.

But Tamara reached up and grabbed

McKenzie's long hair, pulling down hard. McKenzie screamed. She reached down and started to pry off Tamara's fingers. As she did, Tamara reached up with her other hand and raked her long nails across McKenzie's cheek.

McKenzie staggered to her feet. Tamara scrambled up also.

"What's got into you?" McKenzie yelled.

But Tamara wasn't listening. She lunged, clamping her hands around McKenzie's throat. Tamara's long nails were digging into her neck; she couldn't breathe. . . . McKenzie fell backward, and they toppled over together. That broke Tamara's grip. Now they rolled over and over across the floor, clawing at each other. McKenzie began to kick.

That stopped Tamara for a moment. McKenzie got to her feet again, but now Tamara was between her and the door. Tamara slowly got to her feet. Her hair was wild now, her lipstick smeared, her dress ripped. She picked up the desk lamp and slowly raised it in the air. She took a step toward McKenzie. Tamara had her cornered, and she was about to smash the lamp down on McKenzie's head.

chapter 22

McKenzie stepped back. She was up against the wall now, pressing herself against the unyielding plaster.

Tamara's face was contorted with anger as she lifted the lamp higher.

In the split second before Tamara brought the lamp down, a sentence flashed through McKenzie's mind:

I've got a little data for you to enter.

She remembered hearing Dr. Chaney say it to Tamara. And when he did, her mood changed. Could he be hypnotizing her too? Could that be her hypnotic key command?

Gasping, McKenzie blurted out, "I've got a little data for you to enter, Tamara."

Tamara's head twitched, just once. She hesitated, then she stared at McKenzie vacantly, her eyes glazed.

I was right, thought McKenzie. "Put down the lamp," she ordered. Tamara obeyed.

McKenzie slowly edged away from the wall. "Stay right where you are," she commanded.

Tamara stood still, staring at her with those dark, glassy eyes. Carefully keeping an eye on her, McKenzie bent down and scooped up some of the files. Then she slowly backed toward the door. "Clean up this mess. And don't follow me," she warned.

Then she closed the door, turned, and ran faster than she had ever run in her life.

As soon as she got home, she grabbed the telephone receiver and dialed Lilicat.

As the telephone rang, she opened the files. She riffled through the pages. What? The Music Experiment! No! She didn't have any of the Fear Experiment files at all! In her rush to escape from Tamara she had grabbed the wrong stuff. Now she couldn't prove that Dr. Chaney was responsible for Jane's accident—or anything else.

"Hello?" Lilicat's mother answered. "Hello?"

McKenzie hung up the phone without saying a word. She rested her head in her hands. The last thing she wanted to do was go back there, but Dr. Chaney wouldn't be in his office again until much later, and without those files, it would be just her word against his. And Dr. Chaney was nothing if not persuasive. What chance was there that they would believe her? And besides, Tamara must have left by now. Maybe she had gone to get Dr. Chaney. The last place he would look for McKenzie now was at the lab.

"McKenzie?" her mom called as she reopened the front door.

"I have to go out again, but I'll be right back," McKenzie answered.

"Your father and I want to speak with you."

McKenzie hesitated. She decided to pretend she hadn't heard. She closed the front door and hurried toward her car.

She drove fast the whole way, slowing down only when she turned onto Ivy Lane. She couldn't believe it. There were now several cars parked out front of the lab. One of them she recognized immediately. It was Dr. Chaney's dark green Jaguar.

She put the car into reverse and stepped on the gas. But just then she heard a man's blood-curdling scream. She screeched to a halt. There was another scream. And another.

McKenzie scrambled out of the car and raced toward the lab.

The door to number 241 was ajar. Inside, she found a horrible mess. Everything had been trashed, broken, Tamara's desk had been over-turned.

"Dr. Chaney?" she called. "It's me, McKenzie."

Then she heard the sound of glass shattering in Dr. Chaney's office. She rushed toward it. Icy wind hit her, blowing in through a broken window. She looked out. She was just in time to see a boy climbing down the fire escape. He dropped the last few feet and escaped into the night. The boy was carrying a baseball bat.

It was too dark to be sure. But she thought it was Paul.

Just then a hand—icy cold—gripped her ankle. She screamed and jerked her foot back. When she looked down, she nearly fainted. At her feet, in a pool of blood, lay Dr. Chaney.

chapter 23

"Dr. Chaney!" McKenzie screamed.

He didn't answer. He didn't even open his eyes. Blood was oozing from under his head and trickling down the side of his mouth.

She backed away from him, clutching her head with her hands. She wanted to run. "Phone!" she ordered herself. The phone had fallen to the floor. She bent to pick it up. Then she saw it. From across the room, the beady red eyes of a rat stared back at her. She yelled, but the rat didn't run. Then she tried to punch in 911. Her hands were shaking so badly that it took several tries before she managed to do it.

As soon as they had the address, she hung up and called her dad.

Fifteen minutes later, Dr. Chaney was being carried out of the building on a stretcher. White-faced, he looked more dead than alive.

"Patient is unconscious," a medic barked into his walkie-talkie. "Vital signs are weak. There's been a lot of blood loss."

Emergency medical workers loaded the stretcher into the ambulance as the spinning red siren lights raked over the scene.

Two cops, a thin man and a heavyset woman, were questioning McKenzie. So was the principal of her school. Her dad was there too. He had his arm around her.

"Okay," said the policewoman, whose badge was labeled KUBEK. "So you heard the screams. And then?"

"I ran inside and I heard a window break in the back office. So I ran back and looked out the window."

"Did you see anyone?" asked Officer Martin, the other cop.

McKenzie hesitated. She was sure it had been Paul. But she also knew that Dr. Chaney had treated Paul horribly. He had almost gotten him killed in that fight at the mall. If Paul did attack

Dr. Chaney, it was probably because Dr. Chaney finally pushed him too far.

"I said, did you see anyone?" Officer Martin repeated.

"I'm sorry," McKenzie said. "I'm kind of in shock."

"That's okay," Officer Kubek said. "Take your time."

"Maybe she should talk about this later," Shelby said, squeezing McKenzie's shoulder protectively.

On the other hand, McKenzie was thinking, if it was Paul, he might come after *her* next. He might have seen her standing at the window.

"Look, if you saw someone, you better tell us now," Martin said gruffly. "We've got a possible murder on our hands here."

"I did see someone, but . . ."

"Man or woman?" Kubek interrupted.

"Boy."

"Tall? Short?"

The principal was staring at her. "McKenzie, if you know who it is, you should tell them."

"I don't know for sure," McKenzie said, "but I think it was Paul Kelley."

The policewoman wrote the name down while Officer Martin immediately got on his walkie-talkie with the news. They had a suspect.

It was after midnight. Everyone in the Gold house was sound asleep. Except McKenzie. She was wide awake. Every time she closed her eyes, she saw another horrible image: Jane's accident, Dr. Chaney lying in the pool of blood, Paul with the baseball bat in his hand. She hadn't even undressed for bed.

Finally she gave up. She sat up in bed and looked at her digital clock: ten after twelve. She quietly padded downstairs and stood in the light of the open fridge, searching for a snack that might calm her down. She tried microwaving a cup of milk, but when she sat down to drink it at the kitchen table, her whole body began to tremble.

She got up and began to pace from the kitchen to the living room and back again. It's over, she told herself. It's over. Dr. Chaney was in the hospital. FEAR had indeed turned out to be the password for the computer. The police were going through all of Dr. Chaney's files.

Dr. Chaney was no longer in control, no longer a threat. She was free of him. It was time to get the bad images out of her head.

But if that was true, why did she sense

that she was in danger? What gave her the weird feeling that something was still terribly wrong?

She walked into the living room once more, sat on the sofa, and rested. She gulped down the milk. The hot liquid felt soothing. And she was so very tired. She reached up and turned off the lamp. She leaned back, closed her eyes. Maybe she could sleep after all. . . .

McKenzie opened her eyes. The house was completely dark. She couldn't see a thing. It took her a moment to reorient herself. One thing had changed: she was feeling better. She made her way to the fridge and took a swig of soda. Time for bed.

As she crossed the living room, she felt a sudden draft. She turned. Across the darkened room she could see the white curtains blowing in the wind.

That's strange, she thought. Why is the window open? Someone must have left it open. Then she had another thought, and it terrified her. The window hadn't been open when she fell asleep. . . .

A hand clapped over her mouth. She tried to scream, but it was no use; he held her too tightly.

"Don't try to struggle and don't m-m-m-make a sound," her attacker warned, "or I'll kill you. I swear I will."

She turned her head, her eyes beginning to adjust to the darkness. It was Paul. Holding a baseball bat.

chapter 24

Paul shoved her toward the front door, jabbing the air over her head with the bat. The look in his eyes seemed totally crazed. "G-g-go!" he hissed, and shoved her again.

"It's cold out there," she said, her eyes on the bat. Should she run? Scream?

He grabbed the nearest coat—her father's—and threw it at her. Then he covered her mouth again. "No talking," he ordered, his face twitching. "Go!"

She went. But not outside. She tried to run past him, back into the house. He grabbed her, clutching her shirt collar so tightly she began to choke. He threw her back toward the door.

Outside, she saw he had his car parked out front. He flung open the passenger-side door. "Ge-ge-get in!" he stuttered.

He was wired. He kept darting his head around, as if someone were about to attack him any second. He hurried to the other side of the car, put the bat in the backseat, and pulled out of the driveway.

"Paul," she began, "what's going on?"

"Sh-sh-sh-shut up!" he cried, not looking at her. He was rocking back and forth in his seat, gripping the wheel so hard that his fingers turned white. Nervous energy was pouring out of him.

Okay, McKenzie, she told herself, stay calm. Stay calm? It was hard to believe she was even awake. But she was. Bits of gravel on the floor of Paul's car scratched against the soles of her bare feet. This was a nightmare, but it wasn't a dream.

"You'll feel better if you talk about it," McKenzie said, looking straight ahead. He was doing at least fifty on the icy road. "I know this whole business has had me really balled up. And he programmed us not to talk to anyone about it. But—"

"I said to sh-sh-sh-shut up!"

"I know. But I can't."

He darted a furious glance at her. She could tell he was feeling as much pain and fear as anger.

"The police ta-ta-ta-talked to me, you know," he said. "They asked me a lot of qu-qu-questions about Duh-Duh-Doctor Chaney."

"They asked me a lot of questions too."

He hung a sharp left onto McTavish Road, his wheels screeching. Where was he taking her?

"Yeah, well, I bet they di-di-didn't talk to you the way they talked to me. They're trying to get me to confess."

Shelby's huge coat made McKenzie feel small and helpless. But she couldn't afford to feel sorry for herself. Not now. "What did you tell them?"

"I didn't tell them very much because I don't remember very much. I-I-I went to the lab to see Chaney. I felt like I was losing control, you know—becoming kind of vi-vi-vi-violent."

"It's not your fault. I found these files there tonight. We're all part of—"

"Just shut up! Let me tell this!'

"Okay. Sorry."

They were going up a hill. This wasn't the way to his house.

"Chaney put me into a deep trance. And when I came out of it—"

He broke off; he started rocking violently in his seat and driving even faster.

"When you came out . . . ?"

"I saw Chaney." Paul raised his voice. "He was dead."

"No, Paul, he wasn't. I was there when the ambulance took him away. He was knocked out, but he's going to be—"

"SHUT UP! Don't lie to me."

"I'm not!"

"Everyone is trying to trick me!"

Paul suddenly waved a fist in the air. McKenzie shrank back toward her side of the car. She tried to keep her breathing steady. There was nothing but woods around here. Making a run for it would be impossible.

"And I was holding that bat," Paul finished.

They drove in silence for a moment. "So what do you want with me?" McKenzie said.

"The police told me they have an eyewitness." He glanced at her. There were tears in his eyes. He took his hand off the wheel to wipe at his nose. "I know it's you. I heard you come into the la-la-la-lab and call Dr. Chaney's name. I panicked. I broke the window with the bat and ran for it."

"Paul, I'm telling you, Dr. Chaney is alive. I

called the hospital before I went to bed. He's going to be fine."

Paul wasn't listening. He turned onto Mountain Road. Now McKenzie knew where he was taking her. She knew it in her stomach before she knew it her head. Her stomach turned over. She felt a rush of dizziness and nausea. He was headed for the Cliffs.

chapter 25

Paul parked and made her get out. Apparently, one twenty a.m. on a weeknight was not prime time at the Cliffs. So far, McKenzie hadn't seen a single other car.

"This way," he said, pulling on her arm.

"Paul, I can't go out there. I've got this incredible fear of heights."

But Paul yanked harder. He made her walk in front of him. He was marching her straight toward the Cliffs!

Was Paul so out of control that he was going to kill her? It looked that way. And why not? She was the only witness.

She called back to him, "Can't you see that

he's got you so hypnotized you don't know which end is up?"

He grabbed her arm and spun her around. "What—you think I'm in a trance right now or something? This is me. I'm doing this. *Me!*"

She could see it was true. She stared into his eyes. So much pain and fear. In her mind, the image of his eyes grew larger and larger. And suddenly, it was as if she had gone inside— through his eyes, into his mind.

He spun her around. "Keep going," he ordered.

She walked on, but she no longer saw where they were going. All she saw was a vision of Paul, sitting, wearing headphones, his face a mask. . . .

Paul is under hypnosis in the listening room of the lab. Dr. Chaney is talking to him. What is he saying? She can't hear. Dr. Chaney's voice is so soft, so soothing.

Paul nods. Dr. Chaney goes into his office. And then . . . a loud knock at the door.

Dr. Chaney comes out of his office, Paul doesn't even look up. Dr. Chaney looks surprised. He crosses to the front door. He opens it a crack.

WHAM! The door slams back.

A group of high school kids burst in. They've got baseball bats. Robb Sterfeld leads the way.

They shove Dr. Chaney aside. They start to mess up the place. Robb sweeps the papers off Tamara's desk.

Robb looks furious. He accuses Dr. Chaney of hypnotizing his girlfriend. He says he found her self-hypnosis tapes. He confronted her. She admitted it.

Robb is getting angrier and angrier. He blames Dr. Chaney for Jane's accident. He taunts Dr. Chaney with the bat.

Dr. Chaney backs into his office. Tries to reach the phone to call the cops. But Robb knocks the phone to the floor. Then he swings again, hitting Dr. Chaney on the head.

Terrified, his friends all run for it. Robb backs into the listening room. He puts the bat in Paul's hands, and leaves.

They were only about ten feet from the edge of the cliffs. McKenzie could already see the dizzying drop to the valley below.

If Paul could only see what he knows but doesn't know! McKenzie thought. It's all in his mind but blocked by Dr. Chaney's commands.

She stopped and turned.

"Paul," McKenzie cried, "you didn't do it! You didn't hit Dr. Chaney!"

"What are you ta-ta-ta-talking about?"

"It was Robb Sterfeld."

Paul stared at her uncertainly, his eyes wild, his teeth chattering. "It's not true."

"Did you bring a bat with you to the lab? No. And there was no baseball bat around there. So where did it come from?"

"I don't know."

"Robb put it in your hand."

"How would you know?"

"Trust me!"

"It's not true—I did it, I know I did. Oh, God . . ." Paul hung his head. "You don't know what it's like to get picked on day after day. You get so angry. But I didn't want to take it out on Chaney! He was my only friend. He was helping me."

He began to sob. He dropped the bat. McKenzie made no move to pick it up. "Paul," she said gently. "I think I know how you feel."

She carefully reached a hand toward his shoulder. But when she touched him, he jerked back. "You don't understand at all!" he cried.

He rushed past her. He scrambled over several rocks and was soon standing right on the edge.

He straightened up. Then he turned and looked back at her. In a strangely quiet voice he told her: "I'm going to jump."

"No! Paul! Wait! Listen to me."

"I feel so horrible. You'll never know what this feels like. Never."

He was standing so far away. If only she could make eye contact. But the cliffs. She forced herself to take a step toward him.

"Just come down here and we'll talk."

"I'm done talking."

"Paul, I can't come much closer. Being up this high makes me want to faint."

He covered his face with his hands. "Then go home!"

She took another step. The dizziness increased. I'm in control, she told herself, not Dr. Chaney and not anybody else. Just me. And I am telling myself that I don't need to be so scared. Listen to yourself. You don't need to be so scared. Another step. The wind was blowing hard. The cold air cut her face.

"Paul. Look at me."

He took down his hands. His face was wet with tears, his eyes wild.

"Dr. Chaney hypnotized you in the listening room, right? Right? Answer me!"

"Yeah."

"Okay. When you came out of the trance, where was Dr. Chaney?"

Barely audible, Paul whispered, "In his office."

"But when Dr. Chaney hypnotized you, he commanded you not to leave your seat."

Paul's eyes were pleading now. He wanted to believe. "But how could you know what Chaney told me?"

"Am I right or not?"

"You're right."

"Then come down from there, *now*." She took another step toward Paul. "Here—take my hand."

Paul reached out and took her hand. His hand was ice cold. "Now, very slowly, let's start walking back down," she said.

Gripping her hand harder, Paul took his first step.

And slipped.

Paul fell off the cliff. And he pulled McKenzie right along with him.

chapter 26

McKenzie screamed on impact, but no sound came out. She lay facedown on a narrow ledge of rock, her legs dangling over the cliff. Stunned and breathless, feeling as if she'd been punched hard in the stomach, she looked up. She'd fallen, she saw, about five feet.

"McKenzie!" Paul's voice was a terrified gasp, his face contorted with fear and effort. He had fallen farther than McKenzie and was clinging to the ledge with his arms.

"McKenzie!" he cried again in terror. "We're going to die!" And then he slipped a few inches.

McKenzie steeled herself. She couldn't panic. She *wouldn't*. "No, we're not," she said, trying to keep her voice from shaking. "We're not going to die. Just hang on."

She clung to a rock with her left hand and groped for a better hold with her right. She found it, and gathered her strength. Please! an inner voice begged as she kicked her leg up onto the ledge. She fought for breath. She fought to control her nausea. Then she hauled her other leg up.

"McKenzie!" Paul shrieked. "Don't leave me here!"

She reached for him and grabbed his arms. "Don't worry, Paul," she managed to say. "I've got you." Then she pulled as hard as she could. Groaning, eyes closed, Paul pushed upward. With McKenzie pulling on his upper body, he scrambled the rest of the way onto the ledge.

They climbed up the cliff and lay together on the grass at its edge, panting too hard to speak.

Then he began to sob. Her arms went around him. "It's okay, Paul," she whispered. "We're going to be okay." And for the first time in weeks, she knew it was true. Everything was going to be all right.

A funny thought came to her. She had finally made it to the Cliffs—and with a guy! Though it wasn't exactly the way she or Aidan had pictured it. She laughed out loud.

"What's so funny?" Paul asked, wiping the tears from his face.

McKenzie shook her head. "It's nothing. I'll tell you about it another time."

Then she led Paul back to his car. "I'll drive," she said.

"Where are we going?"

"To the police. We're going to have to tell them about Robb."

"Are you sure we should?" Paul asked, startled. "What if he comes after us?"

"I don't think we have to worry about him," McKenzie reassured Paul. "We have to explain to the police who's *really* responsible for what happened to all of us. Everything is going to be okay. Dr. Chaney won't be able to hurt any of us—ever again."

epilogue

When McKenzie opened the door to the gym, class was just starting. Everyone was lined up, and Ms. Lyons was talking about the day's program.

Then she saw it. By the scoreboard. The rope!

McKenzie stared at it silently. Then she took her place in line next to Lilicat.

"That rope sure brings back a lot of bad memories," Mack whispered to her friend.

Lilicat rolled her eyes in sympathy. "Are you ready for Thursday?"

"I guess," answered McKenzie. "Robb's trial shouldn't be too bad, since he's already confessed to the whole thing. But I can't believe that in another few months I'll have to go through it all over again—at Dr. Chaney's trial." McKenzie and Paul—who was doing much better now that he was working with a good psychologist—would have to testify in both cases.

"The third captain for today," Ms. Lyons was saying, "is—" She checked her clipboard. "Jane Ewing."

Jane trotted out to stand next to the gym teacher. McKenzie caught her eye and smiled.

"What are you going to do?" Lilicat whispered, nodding her head in the direction of the rope.

"This time I'm going to make it all the way up—and fast," McKenzie answered with a grin.

Lilicat looked shocked. "Now ask me if I'm scared," McKenzie added.

"Are you scared?"

"Petrified!"

They both laughed. Then Ms. Lyons blew her whistle, and gym class began.

She's got—

THE
POWER

by Jesse Harris

At first glance popular, pretty McKenzie Gold might seem like just another teenager. But her family and close friends realize that there's more to Mack than meets the eye. Only they know about her psychic abilities—the visions, the premonitions…the Power.

Now you can join Mack and her friends in thrilling adventures that test her supernatural powers to their limits. Read them all, and decide for yourself—*is it a gift or a curse?*

#1   *The Possession*   #4   *The Diary*

#2   *The Witness*   #5   *Aidan's Fate*

#3   *The Fear Experiment* #6   *The Catacombs*

First time in print!

Borzoi Sprinters published by Alfred A. Knopf, Inc.